UNIVERSES

Ndu Paul Eke

Kidding in a Theatre of War

© 2023 **Europe Books**| London
www.europebooks.co.uk | info@europebooks.co.uk

ISBN 979-12-201-3734-8
First edition: March 2023

Kidding in a Theatre of War

A story based on historical events.
Many of the names of persons, institutions, communities and towns mentioned in it may exist, yet it's a fictional work.

To the memory of many children and young people whose lives got cut short by the war and, the fortune of survivors.

And to those of Mazi Jacob Eke Ugorji & Mrs. Lucy Ebuonye Eke Ugorj, my dear parents.

The urge to tell this story stayed long with me. That helped for research and inputs of friends, family, professional colleagues and others who relished the idea.

Providentially, the year of Covid-19, 2020 through to 2021 further helped the crystallization. Now, all the support has become evident.

I note the days of conceptual guidance provided by Crispin Oduobuk, an Editor and writer of note. The initial critique provided by Justina Eze Onwuneme, Simi Dabup, Blessing Felix Onyemenam, Gift Chinyere Odionye and Favour Ugomma; and those of my children, Bundu Temitope Zoe and Chioma Miracle. The feedback has been helpful. I am equally indebted to Seyi Odewale for her kind support and informed review.
My friend and classmate, Eric Igwebuike Emeka and his 'gang,' gave a fillip to push this work through; the help I couldn't find any other place. I am so grateful.

Then enter the Europe Books team - Francesca, Marialaura and Rachele D'Alelio. They have been generous with the guidance and the midwifery work for **Kidding in a Theatre of War.**

Eternally grateful to God, and for all of you that He sent to my way. You have played your roles well.

Ndu Paul Eke
Refuge Court, Abuja - 2021

Chapter One

The spectators pulled towards the scene like people being goaded. Fifty or more in number they were in their course, some hesitated but continued. Earlier, they had stood on the sides of a major road to peep — Ngwa Road about 150 metres away from the scene. Ngwa Road separated the more developed side of Aba town from the sprawling Ama Mmong slum, they were headed to.
On the side of Ama Mmong, about 100 metres away, another group of young people about the same number had responded to the same scene from where a rousing noise rose and ebbed; it was on Victoria Street, one of the arterial ways into this large expanse of settlement, Ama Mmong. The number of people going to the scene kept gathering. As they arrived, on the spot were other young men and women, boys and girls stretching and climbing pedestals to get a view of the happenings. Some tiptoed to behold a show that seemed to be wowing the people. Then one elated resident on the Street, Uduma, perhaps one of the minders, was already announcing, "this is our own junior Olympics; we know how to do it;" his voice partially drowned by the rousing noise. But he had caught the attention of some, all the same. Some of those spectators pulled towards him and listened awhile to the chest beating stories he told but continued to see the real deal.
Typical Aba spectators they were, good at gazing at such scenes and thereafter tell endless tales. Some residents knew them as *"Aba-n'anya"* people. A nickname that had become a popular descriptive and indicator of the many scenes that the town often spinned. Yet another set of the

spectators had climbed on top of chairs, packs of moulded cement blocks and elevated pavements in front of the bungalows. Their heads seemed to reach to the roofs — dark brownish rusting corrugated iron roofs that looked like canopies to catch a glimpse of a boy everyone hailed. A number of people had joined hands to lift up Emeuwa onto the shoulder of a tall young man. Surrounded, neighbours and spectators took turns to embrace and touch his small head in admiration.

A few minutes ago, the wonder boy dusted other runners in a street competitive race. He won the six-monthly 100 metres race for children in the neighbourhood; against some competitors thought to be older by a year or two.

"Hope you'll grow and become a champion of our Eastern region, and then Nigeria. You'll go to Lagos, our federal capital," one of the admirers prayed.

As they rained those praises on the little boy, Emeuwa, he mopped at the people and only raised his tiny hands intermittently to acknowledge the praises and applause. Somebody had encouraged and showed him that was the right thing to do. He was grinning, rolling his shining eye balls as he savoured the sweet moment of victory.

Some minutes earlier, his cousin, Orji, was with those who made the declaration about his victory. They clapped and hailed as he busted forward to brace the rope before others, the one that served as an end-of-race tape. Some of his adult neighbours on Victoria Street enthused how his performance supported the popular view that he was "a star in the making." Emeuwa competed altogether with 15 other children for a race staged on the dark clayey, undulating Victoria Street, part of the table land known as Aba. The competitors included such peers as Tijani, Tope, and Omokhinovo, Priye, Uche and others. Orji, one of the key organisers was explaining to a group of spectators how representative the competitors were; "nearly all the tribes are here."

"We mingle well; their parents owned some of the houses on the street," Orji confirmed.

In the third quarter of 1965, when the races took place, all the competitors were either in primary one or two classes of basic education school; most of which were government-owned and located across Ngwa Road. Orji put their ages to be between six and seven years.

He had worked with others, some in secondary school as he was, to set up the show. It was a past time activity to mentor younger ones. But over the years the competition had grown in reckoning and was drawing the huge number of spectators thronging the street. Parents were known to have worked hard to enrol their children and wards to participate and helped to finance the event. Orji spoke about how they also assisted with negotiating temporary closure of the street against vehicular movements during the competitions.

On the sides, Rasaki, another of the organisers had started also to talk. "This is why Victoria is different. We're number one; soon these boys and girls will rule Aba sports, even Eastern region." Nengi from Emejiaka Street retorted; "and so...?" Rasaki looked in his direction, "well, we're building our neighbourhood, helping to raise a better generation. We're proud of it." He moved on thereafter. Ikeogu from Onyebuchi, one of the neighbouring streets pulled Nengi to himself. "Forget these people; they keep talking as if they're the only street in Ama Mmong." Apart from Emejiaka, Onyebuchi, Arondizuogu and Agharandu Streets were also close to Victoria.

For all the fanfare and attention, the athletic show always generated, the people regarded it as only less significant compared to the annual masquerades dance during

Christmas and Easter celebrations led by R.B. Albert and Akataka.

"Everybody here isn't from Victoria," Orji told one of the spectators.

"They come all the way from Ibere and Ibadan Streets," he affirmed. Ibadan and Ibere, further down the section of Ama Mmong were almost one kilometre away.

Qualifying for the final race had stretched for one week and through two other levels before the final. Six children ran the last race which Emeuwa won. At the crowning ceremony, one of the parents presented mementoes and gifts to the children. Year after year, different parents took turns performing the ceremony of presentations.

Emeuwa got two pieces of ceramic cups branded in the green-white-green Nigerian national colours, a flag in the same design and a pack of candies in the current year's contest.

"They are leftover mementoes shared at the celebrations of Nigeria's political independence in October 1960" Orji said.

The boys who took second and third positions were rewarded with whistles and handkerchiefs in the national colours of Nigeria.

Unlike others, Emeuwa had just started primary school. Earlier in the same year, 1965, he was refused admission into primary one at the L. A. Primary School, Ulasi Road, Aba, about 750 metres away from Victoria Street. The school administrators argued that he was under-aged. But his father, Amadu Okocha thought that his son's sporting abilities and native sense could have given him some advantage.

"He runs domestic errands well; think he'll cope in school too," Okocha had added.

He had a comparison to make. "Is there any real difference between five and six-year-olds? They can all be in the same class. In my hometown, Amaeke Item, some are in the same age-grade with people older by about three years," Okocha continued.

His Amaeke people ran a compulsory age grade system for local administration and community development. Young people every four years at the age range of 30 -33 years formed themselves into a group and chose a name as a specific identity. But then at about 70 years or more, the particular age grade retired from community work and graduated to the class of community elders.

Okocha's arguements didn't seem to have moved the school officials to his side. They had added another qualification to confirm Emeuwa's eligibility. He "must stretch his right hand across his head to touch his left ear lobe." But his hand couldn't touch his ear.

Papa Emeuwa chose to try another school. He must clock more distance to get there. He and his son moved on. Papa put Emeuwa on his shoulder some of the time to get there or walked him to cover 300 more metres to reach the Methodist Primary school. He got the same response. Emeuwa would be six November 1966.

"Some of his mates are in other schools already," Okocha had pleaded.

He left the school premises and headed to the Church District headquarters on Azikiwe road at the city centre, to lobby. They had a record of his credentials as an active member of Methodist Church, Nigeria.

The church office checked his records with them — baptismal record, class attendance, membership of numerous church societies and payment of class fees. Okocha was said to have been marked upto date and qualified for some kind of a "waiver" for the admission of his son to the school. However, the admission would be on "probation," the Methodist school leadership insisted. The same year, 1965, Emeuwa started in primary One A.

He spent only a term of three months at Methodist before Okocha sought and got him transferred to L.A. Primary school, Ulasi, which was his original choice.

In the Ama Mmong community, especially on Victoria Street, Okocha had become one of the notables. He first lived there as a tenant having relocated to the place early in its development and participated in the communal efforts at paving the roads, filling up swamps and clearing some bush parchments. More so, he was said to have settled in Aba as far back as 1936 after he migrated from his Amaeke Item village, up north of Eastern Region, in Umuahia province, Bende division, to join his elder brother, Ottah, as an apprentice trader.

Done with the apprenticeship, he launched out on his own choosing to be an itinerant trader. Aba - Lagos route was his first choice. Okocha's textile retail business blossomed in a short period but was cut short by an automobile accident at a notorious corner on Ijebu Ode - Ore section of the road going to Lagos. The bus had somersaulted after it dodged hitting another bus that fell into a big pothole.

"Of the ten passengers in the Ford bus carrying us, only me and one other man came out alive; only God knows how," Okocha reported. He was bed-ridden for about one month in the hospital where Doctors battled to restore his health.

The news filtered to his dear mother, Ulo Elu Onye Aku in his hometown. Ulo Elu, a widow, was said to have feared for the worse for her favourite son.

Those who went to break the news to Ulo Elu would battle to resuscitate her after she collapsed on hearing the

news. A retired nurse was said to have been invited to help revive her. When she regained herself, she kept asking, "Did Amadu survive?" A few days after, she summoned family members at which she deposed, "If he wants to see my dead body, let him continue to travel to Lagos." Okocha's itinerant trading stopped abruptly. He wouldn't take any steps to upset his dear mother.
"I settled, found another business in the Aba city and never travelled to Lagos for business except on visits," Okocha said.
His new business of sewing and retailing a velvety cotton material nicknamed *Polo* had begun to grow and bloom. Thoughts on how to develop the plot of land he bought in 1956 had taken over his mind, the one that was now on Victoria Street, near Ngwa Road. Okocha soon hired brick layers to mould blocks for the construction of a bungalow.
Baba Rasaki and Baba Tijani were the first to visit him at his site when he started. The two owned No. 7 and 11 Victoria Street, respectively. "In few years from now, your property would've gained much value," Baba Rasaki had told him. "That's why some of us came here," Baba Tijani concurred. Baba Rasaki, a Yoruba had lived in Aba for more than 20 years while Baba Tijani, a Fulani from Yola relocated from Enugu to Aba in 1950.
Okocha completed the construction of his 8-room house late in 1959 and moved in 1960. There he joined others to celebrate Nigeria's political Independence on October 1, 1960. It was in the same building that Emeuwa was born about a month after the celebrations. At birth, Mama Emeuwa was said to have held special thoughts about her newborn son. She only would smile at people who spoke in agreement with her thoughts.

One of the tenants at No. 8 Victoria Street, Egbuta, was fond of Emeuwa and wouldn't stop to talk about how he "grew faster than his mates and did things beyond his age."

Emeuwa was coming of age, playing on the Street and often joined others who ran in the rains, the pounding rains of Aba.

"Lots of fun to float on the street flood. Everything provided a plank for play and pranks," he enthused.

In January 1966, things had started to change. "Some days into July, we didn't play a lot; some of my playmates would come out, others won't."

He and a few others would reason that their parents didn't permit them to go play. But for weeks, it continued.

"On their pavements, they showed up sparingly and wave at us while we passed," Emeuwa said.

It continued for days and into weeks. Soon, it looked like other adults in his vicinity were also reacting to the same information as those children and their parents. More and more they gathered and discussed in groups in an agitated manner.

"In the evening, one of those days, tenants in our yard and Papa surrounded a transistor radio. They are bending and lowering their necks, their heads touching each other near the speaker of the radio. After, they said that a coup happened in Lagos."

Some of the adults asked the same questions some of the children were asking — "coup d'etat, what is the meaning? One of the tenants, Uncle Raphael, the one that always explained things said it was "army take over; soldiers have taken over the running of government in Lagos." Raphael worked in local government administration headquartered at the Aba Town Hall and often read newspapers for other tenants.

The story continued that "some soldiers killed some big, big people. Another day they said they were looking for the Prime Minister, Balewa after listening to the news."

Days were adding up quickly as it were. Around the street, some of the adults sat or stood, discussed in expanded groups. Their faces looked like that they were having a quarrel, but they didn't exchange blows. They talked, argued and dispersed. Those who looked more educated leafed through newspapers, spoke as if they had more information about what was happening. Some of them were traders, others worked in local government offices and other places.

Some residents had begun to anticipate that a national trouble might be brewing. Nobody was sure of anything, but it looked as if the year was running down so fast.

"Since that January incident, I hung around the groups of discussants, especially those who came around our house; I wanted to know what was happening," Emeuwa said.

"In July, they said another coup has taken place; that this one might cause a war," Emeuwa's Uncle, Agbai was said to have remarked.

"It is a counter-coup, he kept saying."

After the July coup, the meeting of those discussants became more animated. From them, imaginations grew wings. Most people didn't hesitate to contemplate the consequences. Everything looked ominous with hearsays and rumours filling the gaps.

"Okom Agbai, came one evening to tell my Papa that they have found the body of the military Head of State, General Ironsi; he was declared missing after the July coup."

In a few days, Agbai brought newspapers to Papa Emeuwa with reports of massive killings of people of Eastern Nigeria origin in Northern Nigerian cities. They would lift up the papers, turn it this way and that way and sigh countless times. Agbai was now standing and stomping his foot repeatedly.

"See, West African Pilot says it is a pogrom, genocide unprecedented in Nigeria, in fact."

"They have finished our people, they have; every Igbo person, all the Easterners in the North are gone...*Chai. Chineke Ekwola*, God forbid."

The next moment they had run to the radio, listening and shaking their heads vigorously amid sighing so loud.

"I know Nzeogwu and his friends were said to have killed their Premier, Bello and other big people but it wasn't us that sent them; nobody sends soldiers, nobody knows what they are doing," Agbai continued.

What started with the soldiers had spiralled into civilian communities and was promoting hate actions of all dimensions including killing; members of the various ethnic groups laboured to defend or justify and support evil that was going on.

"I heard that they are shouting *Araba* in *Ugu Awusa, in the North*, they want to go away from Nigeria and form their own country."

"If they go, will it stop the killings; must we kill ourselves? Okocha asked.

Emeuwa had continued to look forward to having his playmates join him and others on their turf.

"For days, I wouldn't even see anybody from the houses of Baba Rasaki and Baba Tijani, not even at the verandah of their houses. They won't come out to play."

"Think, as the Easterners ran and returned to the East from the North, the Tijanis and Rasakis might have gone into hiding or taken off back to their ancestral regions in the West and North. I didn't know what happened or didn't."

The movements from the North to the Eastern Region and from the East to the West and North weren't any longer for business or in the normal course. Tension, fear, anger and a foreboding sense of retaliations fuelled them.

Then, news of killings, destruction of properties, and negative disruptions of businesses and economic activities that hadn't been experienced in Nigeria before; most of the older people kept saying, "unheard of, never before, never."

Papa Emeuwa had many of his customers who came from the North. They couldn't travel to the East and sales had begun to drop very fast.

"This thing isn't going to be easy. My customers said that they had to turn back at Makurdi," Papa said while reviewing situations in the yard as they gathered again to listen to news on the radio.

The voices of those singing, "If they don't want us, let's be on our own," had multiplied and gained traction. They even rose higher every time they listened to the news on the radio or bought a newspaper.

By March 1967, on major roads in Aba, demonstrations by students, civil societies and other pressure groups had grown to daily performance.

They were bemoaning hostile treatment of the Easterners in the North and other parts of Nigeria and agitating for separation.

"They don't want us; let's go and be on our own," many of the speakers concurred. Some of the demonstrators carried high printed posters; others had handwritten ones on cardboard papers.

They sang new songs and compositions of solidarity. Many were composed, learnt, performed and circulated to nooks and crannies of the region. If you hadn't learnt to sing them, you could be a suspect. School teachers taught some of them and the regional radio station made them more popular. Established artists lent their voices to the songs.
Sometime in the month of June 1967, Okom Agbai visited Papa Emeuwa again. His visits had been most regular in the last few months.
According to Emeuwa, Agbai was demonstrating to his elder brother, Okocha how people went into long jubilation on his side of residence further down Ama Mmong, after the Leader of Eastern Region, Ojukwu, announced the secession from Nigeria and formation of another country named Biafra Republic.
"But the federal government in Lagos is threatening fire and brimstone... Gowon said that the federal government would do police action, and, in few weeks, it will be over," he added.
"Hope this thing won't become a war ooo..." Agbai said.
On or about July 6, Agbai ran to Okocha, *"agha ebidola;* the war has started. Federal troops are firing at people in Gakem, near Ogoja."
Soon it had reached Oboloafor, then Nsukka, Bonny etc. Nigerian federal troops had started to bomb important cities in Eastern Nigeria — Enugu, Onitsha, and PortHarcourt and, Aba which was regarded as an important centre of commerce and custodian of Igbo political will of a sort.
First bomb attack and the second on Aba, some residents began to relocate members of their families to the ancestral homes in the hinterland.

Nobody thought the war would go beyond the cities.
Early 1968, Mazi Amadu Okocha followed with the evacuation of part of his family from Aba to his Amaeke Item, about 90 kilometres away.

Chapter Two

On that long-stretched Ngwa Road, crowds of various sizes had formed disrupting vehicular and human movement. Cars and Lorries crawled intermittently after parking for upwards of 30 minutes or more. Those walking bumped into each other repeatedly. Now, some complained, peeped, asked questions to find out what could be the cause of the jammed traffic only to behold milling hundreds of protesting students. They had busted into their space from every angle, stomping, shouting, and singing – *nzogbu, nzogbu, enyimba, enyi, nzogbu enyimba enyi...* Some, on a long, straight line, others mingled with other road users on both sides of the road, marching on or gyrating.
As they swerved and danced through their way, a large crowd that followed them cheered. Some of those had something doing around the road and its many commercial outfits. Others had come from various sections of Aba city where the student demonstrators had been and even from the adjoining streets to Ngwa Road. Emeuwa and mates were among those who hurried from nearby Victoria Street to go watch the scenes.
The protesters, a coalition of an army of students from various secondary schools in Aba, were adding their voice to the growing public support for their new nation, Biafra. But the march had all the trappings of a fanfare. As the demonstrators bounced along more people trooped to the road to join the already excited groups of spectators.
Papa Emeuwa, Mazi Okocha who ran into the demonstrators on his way back from Ekeoha market said that other

sets of students were marching along Tenant, Hospital and Ehi roads apart from the Ngwa Road group.

"Well, they have been at it even before the Eastern Region became Biafra," he added.

Much of those had followed the military coup of July 1966, the second that year or the retaliatory one as it turned out to be.

"They can't continue to kill our people in the army; it's enough," some of the demonstrators said on the sides. They stopped at some places where larger audiences formed, to make angry speeches extempore. War mongering shouts of slogans they mouthed intermittently. They didn't hide their support for the secession of the Eastern Region from the Nigerian federation and the ensuing war.

On the sidelines, Emeuwa watched, grinning. His school mate, Uche was with him as they gazed at the fullblooded young adults. "I like what they are doing," he said to Uche." They laughed and continued to watch the students jumping up and down. "See my big sister, Ugo; *haaa* see Dee Eke, my cousin, they are always there." Ugo, a brilliant student and exemplary, was everything Emeuwa wanted to be.

"They represent our family," he continued.

The two were students at the Eastern Commercial Secondary School, waterside, Aba. They appeared along with others in white T-shirts, khaki shorts or skirts, and white sports shoes — chanting, singing all they could.

Their favourite song was "We Shall Not Be Moved" -

"We shall not, we shall not be moved
Just like a tree that's planted by the waa - ters
We shall not be moved... [They bellowed the last line in unison]
We shall not be moved; Biafra wins the war..."

The student demonstrations had invited multiple reactions. People formed themselves into various groups to herald what they were doing and compete with songs and compositions. Some suggested that some of the songs had been lifted from the many training depots of Biafran Army recruits. "They aren't for 'idle' civilians," one of those had said. Whatever, the civilians were expected to cheer from the rear even if they had to struggle to sing along. To sing the solidarity songs, everybody did anyway.

"Every time I heard or sang those songs with them, emotions rose right up in me, not only me; we'll start behaving like those demonstrators, mimicking the fighters we see in photos," Emeuwa said.

As the days rolled by, road demonstrations were not only done by students. Other able-bodied fellows had joined, sang and gyrated on the roads and streets and neighbourhood open spaces. Their rendition of songs compared well with those of Negro blues of the foremost African Americans.

Here they were, the new Biafrans showcasing their support for the new republic; one they claimed had much better promise. It had just come into existence on the 30th of May 1967.

From the various residential belts, you couldn't count the number who trooped to the streets daily and marched through those open spaces and fields. Only then, the elderly would take turns to exhort them to be steadfast.

"You are laying claim to your new Biafran identity and doing so publicly," a voice rang out.

"You are partaking in the Biafran struggle from the rear, okay?"

It might well be that some of them would get to the war front in the near future.

At a corner, some young people stood and watched, not knowing whether to join or be spectators of the conviviality that coloured the public protest. They were approached by some of the elders, who appeared to be watching over proceedings.

"You can't stand idle in this matter; this is our Biafra; you have to join. Do whatever you can, *unu anula, have you heard?*"

More groups were joining the people already out, bringing dimensions to the show. One of such sang crying, with a rare invocation of emotion, mimicking persecutions and the pains some Easterners had experienced in the North and other parts of Nigeria.

Yet another group that arrived with their musical equipment began to sing melodious songs that stirred not a few.

"You will listen and forget that war causes death and destructions," one of the cheering elders said.

Mondays through Saturdays, they marched, and thronged Aba major roads — Azikiwe, Hospital, Tenant, Market, Asa, Jubilee, Ehi and more.

In the beginning, Emeuwa's class teacher, Ihechukwu, taught him and his mates some of the songs. Now all categories of people sang freely, much more than they could sing even religious songs. Everyone seemed to look for something to do, to be seen supporting or working for Biafra, even children.

Some of them had sneaked out to go hang around soldiers or the para-military organizations stationed in some locations.

Emeuwa said that one of their neighbours on Victoria Street, Agbaeze, aged about 13 or 14 was one of the teenagers who sneaked into the training and recruiting depot at Ovom near Aba.

But he returned, sadly, when he was adjudged "underage" and turned back. Yet the authorities couldn't stop some of them who volunteered to be in the *Boys Company,* to do parades, imitate soldiers and perhaps grew to do reconnaissance for them. Some might have strayed and filtered into other amorphous guerrilla organizations, some suggested. Those who couldn't get close to the armed forces joined groups making all kinds of music. Everywhere people turned, they were greeted with a variety of promotional materials orchestrating all sorts in support of the cause of Biafra. The best places of the display were at demonstration grounds or during the road-show like processions.

Some of the days, Emeuwa and family were woken early in the morning by that sonorous singing; "the boys have come again, and they are shouting and bellowing in Igbo:

Ojukwu nye ayi egbe

Eee iwedi'ayi, iwe

Ojukwu nye ayi egbe

Eee iwe di ayi iwe

Ojukwu give us guns, we are angry..." to avenge the wickedness meted to Easterners.

"It's one of the songs of new recruits," they said. The marching and singing would arouse many to join the march around Ama Mmong area covering those streets across Ngwa Road such as Ohanku, Victoria, Emejiaka, Agharandu, Onyebuchi, Ibere, Ibadan, Obohia streets etc. As they sang and danced in the open spaces, another group of motivated elders addressed them. One started slowly and gradually raised his voice in a crescendo of heart-trending vibrations and revamp. Then he summarized:

"You must be relentless and resolved; be in the vanguard to fight to defend your fatherland; you have no other."

As he was finishing, another had taken over. He was on top of his croaky voice. "May I remind you" his voice reverberated in the makeshift public address system. "No power in black Africa can subdue Biafra." Others in the assembly responded, "Ojukwu said so."

Wait for it: everything had gone frenzy. Men and women, young and old screamed and vibrated in affirmation. On top of their voices, they sang more and stomped the ground. Some gesticulated all the way, flexed muscles, ran and bounced as if the war would be fought man to man, woman to woman on account of muscular power or something.

Emeka Ojukwu, a Lieutenant Colonel in the Nigerian Army was the Governor of Eastern Region. Upon secession of the Eastern region, he became Head of State of the Republic of Biafra and a four-star General of its Army. Many Biafrans boasted about his training at the Oxford University and Royal Sandhurst Military Academy in England.

"When he speaks — it's fiery, inspiring, his choices of words, no comparison. His listeners could walk through the walls," Okom Agbai always said.

Not a few universities, secondary school students and other youths supposedly enlisted in the Biafran Armed Forces drawing inspiration from him, the people discussed in pockets of groups.

"Heard undergraduates of the University of Nigeria, with campuses in Calabar and Port Harcourt, had joined the army in droves," Emeuwa said quoting his uncle, Agbai.

As the year 1967 wound down, Nigerian federal Air Force had bombed Aba more than three times. Emeuwa and his mates couldn't return to school.

In no time, the bombs hit prominent places in the city including the popular Aba Town Hall, a local administration centre and city landmark.

Doubts about the ensuing war were clearing rapidly as increased fear and helplessness took over even in the face of palpable determination and courage of the people of Biafra.

Emeuwa and his mates, those still at Aba, couldn't play around. Imaginations were running wild and yet nobody could make accurate guesses of the dimensions it took in months.

Overnight, Papa Rasaki, of the Yoruba tribe sold his house at No. 7. They had since left for their ancestral hometown around Ibadan in the Southwest of Nigeria. Emeuwa's father would allude to Papa Rasaki's push before he sold the house.

"My older relatives stopped sending me to deliver their love notes to the man's beautiful daughter, Kati or so - called," Emeuwa said.

"My errands to the house ceased ultimately after they relocated."

Soon, new occupants, Mr and Mrs Madumere took possession of the house having returned from Kafanchan in the north of Nigeria. They didn't have grown daughters like Papa Rasaki.

As more people arrived, they brought more stories — about happenings in the North and other parts of Nigeria. Additions came from radio news, but hearsay and rumours must have made up for the rest of information. They flew up and down.

"My parents would come home from their shops complaining of no sales, no supplies of materials, and what Nigeria wished to do to Biafra." The other side was what Ojukwu said — "how even the grass in Eastern Nigeria would rise to fight for Biafra…"

Exchange of fire had started to go on in multiple sectors/towns of the Eastern region. In the evening times Papa Emeuwa's transistor radio was out in the bowl of the yard. Neighbours had joined to listen to the news in the now Radio Biafra. As usual, the tenants sat or stood surrounding the radio.

The English news bulletin came first then the Igbo version. Before the turn of the Igbo news bulletin, always 10 or 15 minutes apart, Uncle Raphael had begun to translate from English to Igbo language for the benefit of all. It didn't stop them from listening to the Igbo language version.

"Remember how much attention they gave to one of the English language presenters, Okokon Ndem and his counterpart for Igbo news bulletin, Julius Eke," Emeuwa said. The Igbo news was often prefaced: *"Oko akuko bu Julius Eke."*

In the news, it was about what Ojukwu said and how gallant Biafran soldiers had performed. Moods, like a pendulum, swung to the rhythm of the news content. Some would scratch; hold their heads in their palms, faces squeezed if it was against the cause of Biafra.

Beyond keeping people abreast of happenings, the news and discussions put Emeuwa's family and others on the edge. Sometimes, it precipitated all kinds of rash actions. The government and the people acted in a similar way riding on the tide.

Officers of the Biafran government had started complaining of insufficient arms and ammunitions. They were asking members of the populace to donate whatever they had.

One morning, Emeuwa's father, Mazi Amadu Okocha brought out his double-barrelled gun and cartridges; something he only did in preparation for his frequent trips to his Amaeke Item to attend some festivities or so.

Okocha cleaned, checked and tightened the screws and said, "I'm donating the gun, and cartridges to Biafran Armed Forces."

Most of the tenants hailed him but he wasn't alone in the gesture. Okocha was one of the many early respondents to the strident appeal of the Biafran government to donate arms to the armed forces of the new republic.

Biafran government understandably had created centres of collection all over the new republic. In Emeuwa's part of Aba, it was the large, long Obowo Town Hall on Victoria Street as large as two standard football fields or perhaps larger.

There Okocha went to hand over his gun and accessories and returned with some satisfaction of his contribution "to our Biafra."

Emeuwa sneaked out a few times to go to Obowo hall to watch the people labour to make the donations of all kinds of guns — short, long, shinny and dark. The venue was four buildings away from Emeuwa's home at No. 8 Victoria Street, Aba. The proceedings were almost endless. Daily, the crowd thronged the place from morning till evening.

It didn't take long, "I began to hear that "Nsukka has fallen; Ogoja has fallen, heavy fighting around Bonny…"

"What did they mean by fall?" Emeuwa went asking some adult relatives and a few playmates still around. They were as lost as he was.

They found out and it wasn't good news or those mysteries that could excite. The ground war had started in earnest and was coming closer to other cities in Biafra.

In between, we heard that "gallant Biafran soldiers resisted the approach of "vandals" to Onitsha, killed hundreds."

The sky and the land looked bloodier, men and women gloomier as scarcity, lack, fear and bad news swooped on people in everything and everywhere.

Prices of staple food stuffs — rice, yam, garri, onions, and tomatoes rose as the days passed. Some suppliers especially those from the North of Nigeria and outside Biafra land no longer moved their goods to the markets in the new republic. Fear of being caught in the web of gunfire prevented the shipments.

Easterners who lived in Northern and Western Nigeria took off, and "ran back" to the East in Lorries, articulated vehicles and trains in droves. Emeuwa's maternal relative, Okom Chukwu and the family had just arrived Aba by train from Kano along with others.

His story was prefaced, "oh, we narrowly escaped death; that pregnant woman and husband couldn't. The angry mob butchered them."

"They jumped the fence, entered, and stabbed everybody on sight, old, young, men and women." He wasn't the only one who told that type of story of gruesome killings. "In fact, from what I could see, heard, hundreds would've been killed just in our section of Sabon Gari; can't say what happened in other sections of Kano and the rest of Northern Nigeria," Okom Chukwu said, his swollen eyes dropping blocks of tears.

It didn't appear that things were under control or that the leaders were in firm charge. Precipitate actions, revenge, grandstanding and exaggerations must have filled the gaps left by leaders at all the strata and divides of the conflict.

Early in the year 1968, Mama Emeuwa woke his son and daughter, her two maids and other members of her household; "wasn't so sure of the time but guess that it could've been about 4.30am; was still very dark," Emeuwa said.

Emeuwa's father had arranged for members of his family to be evacuated in batches to his hometown, Amaeke Item from Aba ahead of him. It must be that early.

On arrival at the garage downwards Ama Mmong area, it looked like there were hundreds of other families already there. Each competed for space in the garage that covered many plots of land.

Many Bedford Lorries had been scheduled to convey people away from the city in droves, like an exodus. Each could take as many as forty-five passengers at a go. Packed at one side of the space, the wooden boards were laid low for passengers to climb in. Nobody could say how many of those Lorries would be able to evacuate all the people milling around, discussing and trying to make sense of happenings.

A few minutes ago, older members of Emeuwa's family dragged and arranged so many pieces of luggage in the yard of their residence. Everything was done in the dark or with little lighting. Lots of baggage and luggage were littered at various points. But Emeuwa went to lie down and slept off under the heap of those that would be transported later.

Other members of the family had taken off with assigned pieces of luggage and headed to the garage.

Fifteen minutes or so later, they discovered Emeuwa wasn't with them. It couldn't have been like Jesus did when he stayed back to reason with Doctors in Jerusalem having gone there with his parents, Mary and Joseph to perform the Passover feast in Israel of old.

Some of the relatives decided to wait on the road while Mama Emeuwa accompanied by one other person returned in search of her son.

Behold, Emeuwa was found under those pieces of luggage, cuddling to complete his "sweet sleep."

"Was woken by a heavy staccato of slaps at my back delivered by my mama's right and left arms," Emeuwa said. "Sleep left me or I left it instantly. I never dosed again till we set sail in the journey at about 6.30am to Item."

Many of the passengers stood through the journey while some sat on the laps of others for the trip of about 90 kilometres on largely un-tarred roads lacerated by erosion.

That the lorry broke down four times completed the agony of the trip. An auto mechanic always came from two or three kilometres away to do repairs before the journey would continue.

From time to time, the passengers complained but some would raise their voices to give advice, "nothing can be compared with the safety of life. Aren't we running for dear life?"

Emeuwa said he found some consolation for the torture of the trip in the anticipation of greater freedom he would have to roam the countryside and go play undetected in *Okpokwuru* and *Iyi Elu* streams among other places.

"When the time comes, would they see me come to wash plates, or go buy something from *Afia Eke*" he reasoned.

They arrived Amaeke Item at about 6.30pm but needed another 30 minutes to get home.

"We carried and dragged our luggage for almost half of a kilometre, Emeuwa said.

They were ushered into a bungalow with a reddish wall, perhaps a four-bedroom house. From the other entrances came four other families of relatives from other towns. One Mama said, "all of you will stay here.
I think we were up to 22," Emeuwa reported.

Chapter Three

That day, federal war planes pierced the blue sky of Aba Ngwa in jet speed and thunderous noise. Scare soon enveloped the proudful residents of the city. Many scampered, diving into the open drainages, under Lorries, and under the shade of trees for cover. Moments after the blaze, they crawled out asking each other questions none could answer. Those around Market Road, perhaps the first target, came to the terrifying sight of the heaps of rubbles of the erstwhile buildings that housed the Onyejiaka hospital. The popular hospital, among others, had been destroyed, reduced to heaps of dark smoking rubbles. All, by the balls of fire that had fallen from the war planes, on everything and everywhere in a twinke of an eye. Helplessly, they watched as human beings, metals and other materials burnt savagely in a place that was hitherto for succour.

All around the vicinity were melted walls, mangled hospital beds, carcass of sets of hospital equipment, and the metal rods that held the pillars of the buildings. Everything emitted thick black smoke.

"Noise of war and devastations has come louder and open, so close," some eyewitnesses lamented.

Before that bomb day, most people including children like Emeuwa thought that the war was far away and that his parents discussed what was happening way far from Aba.

"Now the guns boomed at our backyard, tingled our ears not a little and made our eyes see blood, so soon," Emeuwa said.

Sight and sound of the odiousness of war: Nigeria-Biafra. It had begun in earnest. At least for those who lived far away from Obolo Afor, Nsukka, Bonny and Ogoja axes where it had raged for some weeks and months? Some of these settlements were about 240 kilometres or more from Aba. Bonny and Ogoja were nearer.

Levelling of the Onyejiaka Hospital buildings was one big sign. Housed earlier in massive mosaic structures on a large expanse of land at the intersection of two major roads, Market and Mosque Roads in Aba; it wasn't anymore.

So were the scores of patients, in and out ones, medical personnel and others who were in the hospital at the time. Nobody had certain figures of human casualties in the incident. Buildings close to the hospital had been shaken to their foundations where they were spared of total destruction. Onyejiaka Hospital was known for its brilliant medical services over many years and its buildings served as a landmark for most residents or visitors to Aba.

If you ever missed your way coming into the other side of the city after crossing Asa Road, you were often advised to "look out for Onyejiaka hospital; turn right or left or come straight on..."

With the attack, fear grew across sections of the inhabitants of the city and fast served as a reality notice for the ensuing war. Eastern region commercial nerve centre had been shaken to its foundation.

Okom Igwo, a resident in Aba and who also hailed from the same Amaeke had visited the home of Okocha after the bomb incident. He was talking to the people in the yard pointing to savagery - "the bomb severed the leg of a woman; blew out the brain of a man."

"To identify his body was a puzzle, only sorted when some family members made certain from shreds of the clothes the man wore going out from home that day." Many believed that what they gathered as the man's body might not be his. So were many who perished there.

Another was the case of a popular young man who lived at Arondizuogu, two streets away from Victoria Street, the location of Emeuwa's family house. He was popularly known as John Bull though not many knew it was a nickname.

Shrapnel had cut into pieces John Bull's left leg. Medical people couldn't save or reconfigure the leg and had it amputated.

Altogether, the incident successfully cast a huge hysteria over the erstwhile bubbling centre of commerce as might been envisaged by the federal authorities! If the torrents of fire from the Biafran anti-aircraft guns added to the hysteria nobody could tell. The difference wasn't clear.

Enyimba city as Aba was fondly known had been demystified as it were.

As the war planes operated, tens and tens of children wailed uncontrollably, "*Mama mo, Mama mo, Papa mo, Papa mo,*" ceaselessly," groping for help that looked distant.

"Had meandered home from school at Ulasi Road; a teacher, my father's friend, helped me through East End Road joining Ngwa Road," Emeuwa said. At home, "learnt that Anyim and Uche, my other friends whose homes weren't far from ours had run to unknown places."

Down in other parts of the city were Mama Anyim and Mama Uche crying themselves hoarse, groping and hoping to take the school children out of the present danger.

As if they were immune to the bombs that were exploding with some rapidity.

Nigerian federal armed forces had come to enforce one Nigeria policy on the newly seceded Eastern Region, now called the Biafra Republic. Their war planes were executing its charge without mercy and consideration of the civilian population. It could have been the first bomb attack on Aba since the war started in July 1967.

Vehicles and drivers, motorcycles, bicycles and riders fell upon themselves inside open gutters and drainages running away from the sites supposedly bombed.

One claimed to have overheard a scared Police Officer complaining that "never had Aba experienced this kind of disruptions and instant destructions."

"True, the city always had melees of large scale. Not this type," another said.

The familiar were those occasions when the residents in large solidarity groups sang their favourite mobilization song — *Nzogbu, Nzogbu Enyi Mba Enyi* to galvanize a mob to protest or celebrate victories. But not this time and situation, nobody sang, everybody ran. It had taken more than 40 minutes or so.

Biafran anti-aircraft squads stationed at the football fields of the School of Hygiene, and Township Primary school fired relentlessly. If they hit their target or not nobody knew. Yet those war planes flew menacingly across the sky turning it into black. Billows of smoke from destroyed buildings, vehicles, and human bodies choked breath.

Mama Anyim recovered her son somewhere near the East-End Road, one and a half kilometres away from his Danfodio Road Primary school. That was after a search of about one and a half hours.

From there they meandered through backyard ways to home down the middle part of the long Ngwa Road, at Emejiaka Street where they lived.

Uche, his friend, had run northwards from their school that was near the Aba stadium.

In that course, he fell into *"Gota Ukwu,"* the biggest open drainage in Aba where some other children and adults struggled not to drown.

"Gulped that dirty water, not small, managed to swim across to School Road; then headed back towards Ngwa Road," Uche said.

"Was gasping for breath, fell, stood, waited and began to head to Agharandu Street with the help of one Papa."

About the same time, Mama Uche visited a hospital and Police Station in search of her son. She must have visited her son's school, Danfodio, more than three times.

"Ran up to Ukwu Oji Police station, foremost police office, up in the city but no Policeman could answer my queries," she informed.

"Many were as frantic as I was, like trying to understand what was happening."

Policemen and women, and many others seemed to be moving out of the station with speed and without care. If the arrested and detainees were among them, nobody could tell.

Mama Uche continued her search to Nzeribe Specialist Hospital located around Etche Road. It was nearer their home and Uche's school.

"Everybody's just running to sections of the large premises, paying no particular attention..." she said.

"Nurses moved the wounded in and out of the ICU, barely listened to me."

She returned to her home forlorn, sat for about 30 minutes in the front of the building, chatted with neighbours and passers-by to get a clue of what next, she could do.

Later she moved into the main bowl of the yard, her head dropped sideways into her left palm and sank into a forsaken chair beside her apartment. A tenant emerged from one of the rooms to chat her.

"*Maa,* thank God for your safe return! And for Uche's..."

"Which Uche...? I've been looking for him everywhere." Mama Uche answered.

"*Aaah,* he was the first child in the yard to come back; by himself, on his own. Think he's inside."

Mama Uche sprang up and rushed into her apartment to see Uche hiding and shivering in one corner of the living room. They rushed to each other for a warm embrace.

"Are you okay, *Hewuu Chimoo*? *Oh my God...*" she heaved a sigh as Uche cuddled under her arms. She rushed the boy outside to clean him up, and change his wet clothes splattered with mud.

More neighbours had gathered around Mama Uche who was the wife of the Landlord.

"Very fearful; can we survive this?" They seemed to ask in unison.

"Don't know what has come upon us oo, only God knows..." Mama Uche responded.

"Went round and round everywhere today, walking, running in search of this boy; can't imagine..."

"Aba's just like... markets, businesses, shops, offices and others closed with such speed *eeh;* attendants and officers ran for safety." She had started to shed some tears.

"It's like the world has come to an end. All the cars and Lorries entered the road same time, plus human beings. Nobody could move..."

She overheard a Red Cross official who was helping the injured, wonder why people "crowded everywhere, wailing, going nowhere."

Uche had told his mother that the bomb exploded while he and Anyim were having lessons in "our primary 3B class; Mr Ekpeyong was teaching us Arithmetic."

"Our teacher was shouting, take cover, take cover... after, we started to run."

Some of the bombs had landed around Aba Post Office on Asa Road about one and a half kilometers away from Uche's school.

"They sounded like inside our big school compound," Uche said.

About a week ago, Biafran soldiers had gone around schools and markets in the metropolis to warn about "air raids" and advised on how to "take cover" in case the federal war planes attacked.

From the radio in the evening came the news, "no school will be open for now." The Ministry of Education and the Schools Inspectorate Division were quoted to have given the order.

For more than two weeks, schools would remain closed. An unusual thing had happened, it was better to err on the side of caution.

When other Jet bombers hit the town a few weeks after, it was clear they wouldn't return to school, at least in the nearest future.

"I had thought that the war would only be heard on the radio and as reported in the newspapers," Emeuwa said.

"Or like the ones seen in movies often shown at Dandikos and Rex Cinemas on Ngwa Road and Asa Road," according to his senior cousins

The "actors" in those movies provided the greatest theatrical thrills; not so in this one.

The Nigerian–Biafran war actors didn't entertain. They killed, maimed real people, and destroyed real time.

"Thought about how the war plane was different from the airplane we're fond of."

Emeuwa said that when airplanes flew across the sky, it delighted children like him; but not anymore.

The war planes shattered their popular myth that "if you waved and sang happily at an airplane, the pilot might throw down sacks of money or any other goodies."

"*Eropleni tudaram akpa ego,* I sang with other children in my native Igbo language" in furtherance of the myth.

The Jet fighters of the federal troops, noisier than the ones the children knew and sang to, threw down balls of fire.

Soon, more families hastened their relocation to their ancestral villages.

IN MY STORY

One of my stories
Of the dream Bight of Biafra
One of many stories
I shall tell
When the mightier served evil
To hapless, innocent children in their enclave world
At the behest of most of the powers of the world
World powers without conscience, weird

I shall tell
From the bowels of me
And the depths of me
Good, bad, unforgettable
As I journey in this geography
One of the stories in my story

I mourn my dead and the violated
Cry my cry, tell my tensions
Count my losses, learn my lessons
That the living, unborn may learn
To live without hate, vengefulness
And not repeat evil nor stew in its hellishness
No matter the provocations
Never to grow appetite for retaliations

Now I grab with trembling hands
Hands joined to good hands
To nurture a better people
Brimming with love for God and his people
To build, rebuild, refine

Until a great Nigeria is formed in me
And you, our children and generations
Not that I've forgotten there was a country, Biafra
Yes, the older and present one, Nigeria
I shall persist in hope in this Niger area
For justice, equity, brotherhood
Prosperity of its nationhood
And healing of its many wounds
So I tell

Ndu Paul Eke

Chapter Four

On their way from a farm, it happened. Emeuwa didn't know what to make of it or do!
He stood there and stared at his mother writhing in pain on the ground of the path leading out from Amaeke community farmland. More than five minutes had gone, Emeuwa was still mopping while his Mama lay down helpless, gnashing her teeth.
Surprised that she took a fall on the farm pathway, he couldn't guess what else might happen. He hadn't seen her ever fall; lie so helpless on the ground.
"Didn't think it's for real, that it could happen," Emeuwa said later.
From that ground covered with sharp pebbles and dry leaves, she got on one foot first, then the other, staggered. Her face squeezed and turned red and amplified by her Caucasian complexion. With the same grim visage, she gazed at Emeuwa, the only one around.
Next, *"Emeuwaaaaaa,"* she yelled. Emeuwa shot out his eyeballs, shivering and looking at her.
Mama could be exhaling her pains. She couldn't take notice that all the time she laid there, Emeuwa had started to mutter his sympathies, *"gbeka Mama"* in their local dialect. It wasn't good enough for Mama. That cursory sympathy wasn't what she expected, it would appear.
"Ibughi nwa nwoke... aren't you a male child?" His mother had blurted.
At the age of eight, Emeuwa couldn't bring himself to play the macho man to provide that kind of support or even the emotional massage.

"At least, you should've rushed to help me to my feet?" Mama reasoned.
Emeuwa couldn't see that and must have disqualified himself from the role to lift up a fallen mother of five.
"Thought, she often said we couldn't lift her up, if ever she falls!" Emeuwa retorted.
Mama often told Emeuwa and siblings how they wouldn't have the strength to lift her up if ever she fell down.
"I'm the one who would lift you up if you fell. Allow me to eat, I need all the energy food can give, okay," she would say laughing.
If Emeuwa understood the joke it wasn't clear! "Didn't even cross my mind; wasn't thinking about that. Just that I was tired; after tilling the farm ground, running, and hunting grasshoppers, birds," Emeuwa said.
Mama Emeuwa had stumbled from hitting a stump as the two trekked the distance from the farm belt, some three kilometres to their settlement in Amaeke.
They could have been part of the last band of peasants, rather war-time farmers to leave the farm that day. On their way, Emeuwa and Mama had resigned to walking the stretch alone. Sighting a few persons on the same path could be a bonus of a morale booster. As they cast their sight on the way home, it was like the sun had decided to set; darkness stealthily taking over.
Mother and son were seeking to survive the hunger pangs unleashed by the war, particularly now in their ancestral village of Amaeke Item, on the Biafran side, in 1968, the second year of the hostilities.
But Mama's health had worsened with the birth of her new baby. For her anaemic looks and often complaints of lack of strength, some relatives had tried to persuade her against going to the farm. Eight days ago, she had

Emeuwa's little brother, her 5th child. Of the five, only three were alive.

"I don't have an option," she murmured. Hunger was already ravaging the length and breadth of the Biafran enclave! Nobody minded doing anything to produce food no matter how gruesome.

Biafra, former Eastern Region of Nigeria, was suffering a certain blockade by Nigeria government and allies so much that supply of food items and necessities couldn't reach the new republic especially from the seaports.

Nigerian federal government made up of the remaining three regions — North, West and Mid-West claimed to be fighting to maintain the unity of the country, to crush the "rebellion" of the seceding part renamed Biafra.

"This war, we're in is in two parts as I see it. One's for defence, for freedom; the other's against starvation. Everybody is seeing it," Mama Emeuwa had deposed in a discussion with visiting relatives. Like many, she had chosen to fight starvation headlong and went to the farm in a feeble post-natal state.

The defensive war for freedom had started in 1967, that of starvation, months after the exchange of fire intensified. It was crushing every segment of the Biafran population, women and children especially.

Mama's face no longer looked like that of a 35-year-old-plus woman; it had wrinkled like that of a pulverized 75-year-old. Her pale and emaciated body trunk stared everybody in the face. It was evident that Mama's constant complaint of tiredness pointed to body systemic malaise.

Her cries of inability to get adequate post-natal care had intensified and had become a daily lamentation nobody had time and resources to attend to.

At every turn, other people like her groaned, cried, and told similar stories like in a communal lamentation. And now she just could just be clinging to a challenged hope for survival.

"I'm feeling dizzy but need to go to the farm…" she had complained a day ago.

"What will I do with these children if I don't go? If a hen fails to cluck for chicks, how will they eat?" Mama Emeuwa had said. Her staggered steps belied her words.

She was past feelings for the increase in the number of people dying or those struck by strange sicknesses. Her elder sisters who lived one and a half and two and a half kilometres away respectively now visited often in spite of the risks of trekking the main roads.

They weren't better except that they didn't have the pangs of a war-time nursing mother like their younger sister. They might have stopped bearing children.

Mama Emeuwa had told them how she went to the hospital and was informed that "*Dokita* and nurse have joined Biafran Army." That day she returned home and cried all through.

"The other Dispenser," an auxiliary health worker had also disappeared, and nobody could account for his whereabout.

Some of the clinics had become army camps and war offices of a kind. Nobody talked about medical stores, pharmacies or dispensaries any longer.

"I don't know, the Dispensary at Amokwe is closed, come today, and come tomorrow…" Mama Emeuwa further said.

"They said the one at Okoko has a small quantity of drugs, but nobody can pay the amount they are asking for…"

Meanwhile, Papa Emeuwa was said to be "sweating", searching frantically for buyers of some of his assets to raise money for the purchases.

Mazi Amadu Okocha had lost his business and a sizeable part of his assets at Aba. He no longer could do his normal trading of a special textile material, cotton stuff they had nicknamed *Polo*. Selling off his belongings and trying his hands on petty trading was all he could do. Emeuwa thought that his father, Mazi Okocha didn't quite sell in the open market. He pitched to some wealthy persons.
"He often wrapped them in cellophane to go sell to one Maduka, a rich man and in-law who could afford to pay for those chieftaincy clothes."
"I didn't know the other buyers; they must have been Amaeke people too."
Certain traditional wears and "George" wrappers were a kind of asset the people invested in. The older the brand, the higher the value and resale cost.
There were no indications that Okocha garnered enough money to procure the prescribed drugs for his wife's delicate health and new-born baby.
"I haven't had it like this before, post-delivery," Mama Emeuwa said. She had her four children before now and all of them at the Aba General Hospital, one of the best at the time.
Only her little boy, one week and a day old and named Onu was born in Amaeke Item after they relocated from Aba in fright of the war.
Her fall on the way from the farm might, after all, not be an accident.
If she wasn't tired and feeling dizzy, wouldn't she have had a clearer vision? And perhaps would have gathered her body enough not to go to the ground like a log of wood, some relatives reasoned. The scanty brunch they had at the farm at about 2pm was all for that day.

Mama Emeuwa and children, like others, had gotten accustomed to having one meal a day or two on some auspicious days. Right on the farm that day, she had laboured to plead and encourage Emeuwa in spite of her precarious state.

Emeuwa was crying that the meal wasn't enough shortly after they had eaten. "Mama, can't we go home? Must we finish the work today?"

Languid and sluggish they were, drained of whatever energy they drew from the meal, but they were still pushing in the farm.

Mama Emeuwa had begun to preach. She was persuading her son to be courageous and hopeful that "tomorrow might be better." She had previously told some people so who came to sympathize with her.

A while ago, she was also contemplating going home to go cater to her new baby, and her only daughter, Iroanya. They had been in the care of Emeuwa's paternal grandmother. Yet they couldn't hurry home. They had more cassava stems to bury in the mounds though their strength was diminishing. All indicating that mother and son would be about the last people to leave the farm that day.

If Emeuwa and Mama had enough strength to work the farm they could have been in the batch that set out before sunset. As they trekked the now lonely farm path, the moon light was up in the skies. It had risen with its calmness providing some light to save them from further missteps, meandering and stumbling as they headed towards home. On both sides of the bush pathway, crickets and other nocturnal beings animated by the soft light were the only ones singing and making music.

Soon, Mama began to talk, not a little - "this suffering has increased; everything is scarce, hard and against. Now, who knows when this war will even end?"

"Mamaaaaa... thought you said things would soon change for good; that we should be hopeful?" Emeuwa reminded her.

"Yes, but everything has gone bad. Your Papa's running around, can't provide us with those essentials he often did with much ease in the past. If he did, I won't come to this farm like this."

"Nobody knows when we'll become refugees too; look at those ones living at Umunnato Central Primary School…"

"Does anyone even know when their aeroplane will throw another bomb at the market… hmmm; is it that shelling bomb that'll draw out somebody's heart before landing," she remarked.

Crying and sniffing her nose, she couldn't talk audibly any longer. Drawing back bit by bit, now behind her Emeuwa who had gotten a few steps ahead, she continued crying. She always was in the front when she walked with her son; but not now.

"Mama, mama, *obu kwanu ngini*," Emeuwa asked? He didn't want her to accuse him of "not caring enough" as she had implied when she hit a stud.

As he turned to look, Mama who was wiping her tears, trying to clear her face, murmured *"onweghi, nothing."*

Emeuwa asked her again, *"obu kwanu gini, what is the matter*?"

She sighed, "Let's keep moving," she instructed, her right hand pointing forward down the path.

After some moments of silence, Mama said, "I'm thinking about my life *nwam*, what our world has become…

Is this the way we're going to live? Death, hunger, bad, bad news everywhere...!"

"Who knows what may have happened to Joe, *nwannem nta?* He said he was going to fight the Biafra war"

"Nobody hears anything about him! *Odundu, ka onwuru-anwu, dead or alive,* nobody knows," Mama Emeuwa continued to lament.

Joe, Emeuwa's uncle, his mother's youngest brother had joined the Biafran Army. A few times, he returned to see her sister and other members of the family. The last time his family received news about him was about a year ago. Mama Emeuwa looked down again, sobbing as they continued the journey back to home. She wiped her face with a portion of her wrapper and looked up; there were rays of light in the nearby neighbourhood.

"We will soon get home," she announced with some cheer.

Emeuwa didn't seem to get it; he had stopped to adjust the piercing part of the firewood on his head. Mama stopped too, called him his ful lname, "Emeuwadike."

"Mama, I'm here, I'm coming."

Emeuwadike is his morale booster name. The name Mama always called his son especially if he had performed a task well.

"She may now be feeling a bit light, who knows..." Emeuwa guessed.

He waited for a follow-up but didn't get it immediately. He quickly prompted, "Mama, you were saying ..."

"You see, nobody knows tomorrow... anything can happen the way the war's going. If bullets, aeroplane, don't kill, sickness, kwashiokor may," she said.

"Mama, you've been saying to be courageous that it isn't us alone. What of the many things you said Radio Biafra has been announcing and Okom Agbai's news?"

Emeuwa's paternal uncle, Agbai, a much younger man and former Biafran Army recruit was fond of bringing news from BBC and VOA. According to Agbai, "Federal troops are marching into every part of Igbo land; it may cause the war to end soon."

"Yes, instead of you, Iroanya Charity and Onu to die, it's better I go." She prayed. "Mamaaaa, *Chineke ekwola*, God forbid," Emeuwa retorted.

"You're a kid *nwam*, you can't see how things are going… just be vigilant and watch out" she continued.

It wasn't news any longer that more people were dying daily without taking bullets at the battle fronts — starvation and strange sicknesses were adding to the numbers.

Invading Nigerian federal troops taking some Biafran territories had come so close to Amaeke and from time to time appeared and killed suspects in the community. They had taken many parts of Bende division.

The Biafran soldiers having lost positions visited the community in disguise, taking out some accused of being "sabo," saboteurs, and aiding the "vandals" as Federal troops were typified.

Of those, were BOFF members who visited Amaeke community, especially at night. The BOFF people were mostly young men who weren't in the regular Biafran Army but now operated as guerrilla fighters.

Okom Agbai, however, believed some of them were fake, those who used the BOFF as camouflage. He should know having served briefly in the Biafran Army and returned to the community.

BOFF members were never found in any uniform but had a way of walking around with raised shoulders. You could be in their trouble if you failed to take notice and defer to them. They craved all the attention. All their show was when the federal troops weren't around or hadn't visited.

Side by side, the two sets of opposing warriors trapped and trampled on Amaeke, Item.

Mama resumed her talk. "Emeuwadike, whatever, take note, in you is the history of all this; may be, it will be your turn to tell your children and others…"

"Let's continue to pray that God spares our lives to see tomorrow; any day we see, hmmm, is a bonus, but…"

Emeuwa, yet to be ten, was racking his brain to understand his mother's gist of a prompt.

"Wonder what she wants me to do now," Emeuwa soliloquized.

He kept repeating, *"Chineke Ekwotukwa, God forbid;"* thinking through those words.

"Has Mama heard me, or her mind isn't here…"

They kept walking until they got home. Families which had food for that day were already cooking.

Emeuwadike couldn't remember if they cooked dinner except that he kept his mouth busy munching *Odudu*, local specie of beans eaten as snacks. The snack was reputed to fill the stomach and quench hunger easily especially if taken with lots of water.

When morning came a few hours after, Emeuwa was still munching some leftover of the *odudu* on the side of his sleeping mat.

Two days after, he was on his way to a more distant farm with his Papa. Everyone must do something to fight starvation.

They were on a single line, Emeuwa's elder brother, Omeoga and sister, Oyi followed behind their Papa; it was Emeuwa's lot to carry the four hoes to be used and other accessories. He followed after all of them. For the distance, they set out before 6am. They had to do about 45 minutes trekking before sun rise.

"Heat of the sun will drain strength," Papa said emphatically. He always admonished.

To arrive on time, his father led the pace, throwing his legs with all of the strength of a determined man. The response of a 50 something year old, challenged to survive.

Emeuwa's older siblings always tried to match those of their father, who wouldn't brook any lagging behind or excuses.

"Papa should slow down a little; the hoes are heavy on my head" Emeuwa murmured.

He was drawing back moment by moment and now his eyes were full, pouring lots of tearful water. Papa and the rest walked a distance and noticed he wasn't following closely. Oyi, the only female among them traced back to fetch him.

The trekking journey now restarted; Emeuwa was still behind. Sister Oyi had bent over to whisper, "*jisike*, we'll soon get there; see that tall oil bean tree, it's very close to *ala 'yi*, our farmland."

Sister Oyidiya had lived longer in Amaeke Item unlike Ugorji Omeoga and Emeuwa. She knew locations and boundaries that some family members didn't know and could even lead Papa Emeuwa to various portions of ancestral land of *Nde Okocha and Nwokeocha* lineages.

Still crying, Emeuwa continued with them but from the rear until they reached the farmland for the planting of yam seedlings.

Papa Emeuwa marked out the land and gave everybody the number of mounds to dig and arrange. Digging and cultivation soon started in earnest. Papa Emeuwa always insisted that the best job was done before noon.

He had started to shout and threaten to punish anyone who failed to till the ground as fast as he wanted. Nobody dared to disobey him. With tears or grit, you must work. You better take him seriously because his discipline was with vehemence.

Apportionments of the mounds to dig up were Papa, 120, Omeoga, 100, sister Oyi, 80 and Emeuwa, 50 mounds. They would all exceed the number before the set time.

It was now 30 minutes pass 1pm, Emeuwa hadn't done up to 20 units. "You won't eat ooo, if you don't dig up to 30 by 2pm," Mazi Okocha thundered.

"What've you been doing, playing eeh, okay; you're running after grasshoppers, eeh? That's what you'll eat," he continued.

Emeuwa was crying again. He didn't want to miss the brunch of a roasted yam eaten with red oil garnished with red pepper, and salt, if it was available. It was about the best meal around and only served during yam planting season.

The most delicious was the *efu* yam specie, dwarfish, rounded but so sweet. It was often prepared as a delicacy, and one normally doled out by people rich in farm seedlings. People who had plenty of tubers of *efu* yam in their barn were regarded as rich.

Only the chopped-off bottom part was available for food while the rest with the head was planted.

Emeuwa was able to dig up 35 mounds when his father made the decision for them to eat at about 2.30pm.

"You must complete it 50, no matter what…" Papa told him after the meal. Emeuwa went back to work after and dug up 52 in the final count.

"Hamble, Emeuwadike…" his father commended. Hamble was the name of a European his father did business with, in the later years of the 1950s when he started his "polo" business.

Soon, at about 5.30pm they were ready to go back home. Everybody had performed but they would face the drudge of trekking more than four kilometres again to get home. Everyone seemed to brace up for the challenge except Emeuwa.

Okocha led the charge as usual, in the front of the single line. Omeoga and Oyi in suit and Emeuwa who must carry the hoes and a few of the left-over yam heads that must be brought back home. Sister Oyi had volunteered to help him carry some of the items.

This time, their pace wasn't far-flung or fast as in the morning. Yet, Emeuwa was at the back of the row. His nearly nine-year-old legs hadn't become strong enough though they had gathered trekking hours. Omeoga was about four years older than Emeuwa and Oyi, three years.

Chapter Five

"They are now everywhere," Uncle Agbai announced.

He had brought the story of how the Nigerian Federal soldiers had encircled Bende division and taken control of the vast area of many communities. Bende was one of the important divisions in Umuahia province of Biafra Republic.

It was in the last quarter of 1968.

Agbai's story couldn't be disapproved or confirmed but there was that feeling that he knew what others didn't know. Constant flights of jet fighters and bombers, endless gun shots and booming shelling guns seemed to validate his story.

"If the federal soldiers have reached Bende division, they would get to our part of Item town; it is the same geographical delineation," Agbai argued.

Soon, more stories came about how the federal troops stormed some nearby communities to Item and even some villages of Item; nine of them altogether lying kilometres away from each other. Some of them were as far as five or six kilometres away from each other.

Some rumours here and there had cropped up that they had even come close to Amaeke but were yet to get to the core of the community. Months after, indigenes would come to know that though they arrived later, their community was branded "stubborn" by the invading soldiers.

While the federal troops combed other villages, Amaeke people had hoped that they won't come around. They tried their hands on all sorts including divination to keep them away. Amaeke no longer had the buffer of Biafran soldiers.

The community leadership was said to have gathered many indigenous witch doctors and others from other climes to divine. Nobody was certain how the decision to engage the diviners was made. Or whether they volunteered since some of them were indigenes. Like a drowning person clutching a straw, they had begun to cling to anything that could spin hope.

Early one evening, some non-indigenes arrived in Amaeke. These ones roamed but later were guided to certain entry points of the community.

"*Nde Dibia*, witch doctors are having a meeting in Amaeke," the story had gone out. Some children curiously followed up and watched at a distance. Enyidiya, one of them had told her playmates when they gathered at *Ologho* Eziufu.

"Aaah, they've held a celestial and terrestrial meeting ending up in the home of a native prominent witch doctor, Ikoro," another report from one elderly man.

After which those began to parade the pathways leading in and out of Amaeke Item.

"The leader, a member of Papa Emeuwa's age grade, *Uke Nganga* was in front as they marched bare-foot across the nooks and crannies of the village," Emeuwa added.

Their eyes looked scary like one of those images they often conjured in folklore.

In their attire, they combined white, red and black strands of cloth. Some were used to tie across the feathers of white cockerels they held in their hands.

Somebody said he overheard them say several times, "federal soldiers'll not step their feet into core Amaeke settlement."

They could go to other parts of Item but not Amaeke, some indigenes boasted thereafter.

Somewhere else, some people were arguing that there was no consensus for the hiring of the witches and wizards. Okom Agbai thought so too.

"At the first meeting, some of us suggested village-wide prayer and fasting while others muted the idea of involving the witch doctors, I remember" Agbai said.

"Some even suggested that we should go to the federal soldiers to negotiate since Biafran soldiers weren't forthcoming," he continued.

"When they finally decided to call in *Nde Dibia*, I can't tell." Unknown to many people, the witch doctors had started privately in the morning of the previous day and continued till the evening of the second day.

Seven of them that evening held fresh, tender palm fronds in between their dry lips, white and red chalk stripes plastered around the eyelids and brows.

They neither greeted nor acknowledged greetings. Members of the community curiously watched as they marched around like people that had the "power of life and death" in their hands.

That they wore no clothes on the upper part of their bodies added to the drama; on their waist, they tied around "George" wrappers, dangling white, red and black strands like torn pieces.

"Think they wore war head dress, *Okpu Ugbogu*, the traditionally weaved wool in the colours of red, black and white," Emeuwa pointed out.

The roundish head-dress of which protruding fluffy part fell left or right when it was worn was more often part of the attire for dancing the war dance, *Ikperikpe Ogu*. But achievers, elders and warriors commonly wore the *Okpu Ugbogu* to occasions.

Emeuwa had met them at a path leading out of Amaeke to a big river, and then to a bush path through which Amaeke people went to Abiriba.

"There, they spilled the blood of a white cock, did incantations, tore off some of the feathers, danced, twisted like people possessed by *kamalu* spirit, moved on."

A week ago, the Administrator of Umuahia Province of Biafra, Lt. Col. Simeon, a lawyer and an indigene, visited Amaeke as part of mobilization for solidarity with Biafra.

"Everybody assembled at *Ologho* Ezuifu for his address; as trainee members of Boys Company of Biafra, we staged a parade as part of welcome ceremonies," Emeuwa said.

While the meeting continued, soon there were unusual movements around the platform at which some village principalities had assembled.

In about ten more minutes, it appeared that a piece of new information was received. Somebody called it "asignal about the movement of the federal troops." Col. Simeon, on the elevated platform began to hurry his speech.

"Not many of it I recall but he emphasized that *onye nde iro gbara gburugburu n'eche nduya nche mgbobula, you have to be vigilant if enemies have surrounded your territory.*"

Everybody felt the end of his speech was abrupt. He turned backwards with his Aide De Camp and stepped down from the table used as a podium, like one hurrying to something.

A few minutes on, without the usual fanfare, his 404 Peugeot sedan zoomed off heading towards Amaekpu, an inner village in Item. That was his last public appearance before the federal soldiers arrived.

A day or so after, a number of high ground clearance trucks painted military colours carried soldiers armed to the teeth into Amaeke community.

"Smaller land rover jeeps full of soldiers followed; from some of them, the soldiers parachuted," Emeuwa said.

People moved briskly out of their sight, into homes from where they could peep. Nobody would say anything, and no one was ready to have open discussions or wait around.

Movements had ceased; most stayed back inside their thatched roofed, red-mud houses and only peeped through the pint-size windows.

Some had run out of settlements into yam barn areas bounded by bushes and orchards.

"Then came soldiers on foot from many directions dressed in camouflaged uniforms, helmets and covered with leaves-like clothes."

Emeuwa had run to his elder sister's home at *Nde Ifo Nta*, an elevated bungalow from where he and others peeped endlessly. Quite a number of soldiers approached from the path leading to Abiriba; one of those the witch doctors had sacrificed at.

"You see, the federal soldiers've really broken every obstacle including the so-called defence mounted by the Biafran armed forces over Item," Okom Agbai said later.

Right inside Amaeke, they were and dominantly so. Everybody had begun to adjust to life under the watch of federal soldiers. From time to time, they visited in the same way they first entered the community.

Okom Agbai said that the Biafran soldiers whose visits were now at night had promised to do something soon; "everybody should watch out."

After a while, some young men who claimed to be members of BOFF traversed the community in some kind of braggadocio.

"Never saw them carry arms, do anything except to boast of having Ojukwu bucket, *Ogbunigwe* bomb that can finish the vandals…" Emeuwa said.

From time to time, they were in a scuffle with some people suspected to be "sabo." They would harass and take them away from the community to wherever their camp was hidden.

Chapter Six

They arrived in numbers, dishevelled all through; mopped vacuously at everything and everybody. Quite a number apparently hadn't been to Amaeke for many years. As they dragged along big, long, wrapped and unwrapped fat and fragmented sizes of luggage to a corner, some of the contents dropped. They kept repackaging them, moving to a corner at the Amaeke business district. Others held children and pieces of hand luggage. Pockets of crowd had gathered; some people stopped by to look and offer sympathies but many kept moving and minding their businesses. Most people had it that way earlier. Okom Agbai had told Emeuwa that they were a new set of refugees. The two had met the crowd on their way to Amaturu, an outskirts settlement of Amaeke perched on a hill. Another set of people displaced somewhere else and had scampered to Amaeke, Agbai explained. Erstwhile urban dwellers pushing big pieces of luggage wrapped over and some in large bowls. Their rumpled clothes and faces were covered with reddish dust that looked like an excessive face make-up. Rickety Lorries and uncovered cabins had dropped them off awhile ago; some might have come on foot. Nobody cared to know about the towns or cities they ran from except that they looked like others who arrived previously. Their former places of abode had disappeared in the course of an exchange of fire between Biafran and Nigerian federal soldiers.

While they sat at the business district in small groups and waited for help to get to their kindred homes, or a camp, they discussed with a few sympathizers. Some cried that some of their relatives they set out with were cut down by bullets. If the bullets were fired by Biafran or Nigerian federal troops didn't matter. Meanwhile, the refugees that had so arrived thought they were even lucky. "Some couldn't trek on and are behind; nobody can say what happened to them," one of them deposed.

Moments after, the new refugees were beckoning on a hawker of bunches of miserable looking bananas — "we haven't eaten since yesterday; didn't have appetite or time to," they chorused. But they had arrived to an equally traumatized people and a community that was already counting the number of the dead as they occurred daily. It wasn't news any longer that the number had shot up sharply, more people scavenging for food as much as the number reporting sick. Leading those was Kwashiokor, a deficiency disease.

Before them as they waited at the business district were some Kwashiokor patients, with their protruding bellies, swollen legs and watering pale eyes. They were waiting for their turn to be evacuated to the Red Cross Centre at Ozara. Others had died a few hours ago, their bodies covered with loin wrapper on one side.

"I knew some of them even the older ones who passed on in a space of one week," Emeuwa had told Agbai as they continue to Amaoturu clan. Before this new set, a particular set of refugees had come into the village bearing bullet wounds, increasing the scare. Now, some natives had started to talk incoherently — effusive hopelessness and thoughts that anybody could become the next victim.

Papa Emeuwa, Mazi Okocha and younger brothers had so run to Amaeke Item a few weeks ago. They scampered back to the village from Aba about the second half of 1968. Perhaps, were in the last batch that escaped from the city just before it fell into the hands of the federal troops.

Papa Emeuwa didn't imagine that he could trek the distance, Aba to Amaeke in three days; "I mean the whole of about 90 kilometres or more on foot."

They couldn't find enough commuter vehicles to board and resorted to trekking in bush paths and alleys, day and night to save their heads from the bullets.

"Some ran out of strength; those with small children had it really rough… couldn't move much or faster, cried hopelessly. Nobody cared, no time to help."

Some of the transporters had stopped business; it appeared or decided to take their vehicles out of the roads for lack of petrol or out of fear.

Papa Emeuwa and company got to Amaeke with swollen legs, dislocated hips and reddish eyes.

"We didn't sleep for the three days," he said.

Traditional healers daily massaged their swollen legs with very hot water, medicinal herbs, and tingling heat producing ointment. The patients claimed that the ointment was hotter than a popular mentholated ointment known as Hacogen. They had to receive the treatment for weeks or so to regain stability.

As they made bid to escape from the raging Aba battle, they traded some of their valuables in a hurry for money.

"Nobody wanted to risk anything; torrents of bullets flying between the federal and Biafran troops as the former troops attacked Enyimba city with all vehemence."

Influx of refugees from Aba and other Biafran cities continued. In few days, Amaeke had an unplanned population increase. Streams, in full sessions looked like a market with numerous people milling around the banks and in the waters. Some waiting to take turns to enter the stream or just bidding time.

In other public places like the *ologhos,* kindred meeting places, hundreds of people moved around almost aimlessly. Every space had to be competed for by numbers.

Amaeke Item never was so full even during compulsory Christmas homecoming — when the village authorities decreed massive return. They did every four years. A community with an approximate population of about 2500 people grew to more than 6,000 excluding children, and that in weeks.

People were just milling around and couldn't carry on their businesses or any other thing to earn a living. They ran for safety and were content to be back in the village. Civil servants did not have a place anymore to call their office or to go to work, and rarely would one see a moving motor vehicle.

One of those that ran home was reporting how the roads had become avenues of death, and destructions. They had become desolate. "As we head out some days, many now passed through bush and those narrow windy interior paths used sparingly before the war began."

"Didn't see people make telephone calls any longer, Post Offices closed or rendered little services." Communications had become far more traditional — only face to face and not mediated.

"As I run errands for my mother, people gathered in groups every turn, lamented and wished they could make sense out of the massive lack, hunger, deaths and destructions."

Such lamentations soon gave way to survivalist instincts, austere living, farming, petty trading, and game and fruits hunting.

Nobody could ask each other why they emaciated. It was general. That many looked like AIDS patients was common. Perhaps, the group worst hit was those who never lived more than one or two weeks in the village or engaged in intensive and consistent farm work.

"Can't remember all that other people did to survive; my father sold his rich collection of clothes to raise money. Mama followed up selling her *ukpo, hollandis wrappers* and jewellery among others," Emeuwa told.

Everybody seemed to have embraced farming or so it looked but it yielded no immediate amelioration to the "present and biting starvation."

Waiting for the plants to grow and yield appeared too long; hunger didn't wait.

"Mama and I processed garri in one day against the standard three days of fermentation of the cassava flour when you produced it from matured tubers."

Elderly people couldn't question people any longer about harvesting tender tubers like they used to.

"In the morning, it was cassava tiny tubers, in the evening it had become garri with attendant gastro-intestinal rumbles," one Grand Mama had sarcastically told Emeuwa and his mother.

Nobody bothered to follow or respected the well-known village system. Hunger didn't have any respect for the methods that couldn't produce immediate food. Perhaps, that also contributed to the increase in illnesses. The prevalent kwashiokor illness — two out of three children, perhaps, fell to it, a protein and mineral deficiency ailment.

Nobody could count how many days Mama Emeuwa spent on condolence visits to bereaved families whose children were killed by Kwashiokor. Often, she left home for those visits for one full day.

One of those days she had gone to Amauturu, a clan almost a kilometer from hers; from there to her ancestral home, Amauzu and then to Eziufu, her marital homestead.

"Five children were buried that day, just the ones I know," Mama said.

In a few weeks, it became the turn of Emeuwa's younger half-sister, Uzunma. She had been ill lately and frequently too.

Before her legs could swell so much, she was rushed to the Red Cross clinic. Papa Emeuwa had learnt of the operations of a Red Cross team and others in their community. Her admission into the clinic followed a successful "fight."

"Papa entered into a push and shove" just to get her admitted into one of those improvised clinics that littered the premises of Umunnato Central School, founded in the 1940s." It was the only one serving the community at the time.

The three days struggle yielded, and she was taken in. Like a miracle, in about one week, she began to regain her health. All the symptoms – extreme emaciation, swollen legs and hands began to disappear one after the other.

Three weeks after, she was back at home. Her bed and corner in that clinic were up for grabs and could only be obtained by a fight involving five parents.

The Red Cross, with all its zeal and collaboration with other charity organizations, never seem to have enough for all the people who needed urgent attention.

In and around the school premises were long queues of needy, sick and emaciated people. Others spent time under the shade of many trees in the large compound and other humanitarian serving points.

In the queue one of the days, a man took a deep sigh, and dropped to the floor.

"*Omekwa, Omekwa… it has happened again...*" those standing chorused.

They rushed to him to try their weak hands at providing first aid. Shortly after the victim was able to sit with the intervention of the medics; opened his eyes and took some liquid. He had to be served while under the watch of the medical people. Everybody wanted the organization's nutrient-dense corn meal garnished with other therapeutic condiments.

Others in the queue who might still have strength and standing began to hiss and murmur in unison, "when would this end?"

Caritas group of the Catholic Church, World Council of Churches often worked from morning till night to complement the Red Cross in providing those reliefs.

According to some elders, "these charity workers are taking risks; you think Nigerian Army wants them to come here?"

"They are risking their lives for the sake of humanity and God."

This much was readily gleaned from numerous complaints and rumours circulating around the venue and outside.

However, hopes were rekindled that most of the sick could recover by eating Red Cross rations. Many did without further medication. So much like magic, it looked.

Likewise, many who weren't manifestly sick kept vigil and in long queues in the large school premises, under the shade of large and tall trees for the meals to ameliorate their starvation.

That war of any kind was uncontrolled devastation had become common knowledge, the ruin touching lives and materials. Even the kids who had become the most vulnerable must brace up and kid along for survival.

People kept talking about "blockade, blockade" every time the issue of the ultra-starvation and scarcity of supplies came up. Some of the elders were talking and swearing how it won't bode well for the government in Lagos for levying an economic blockade against Biafra.

"They don't really care about human lives, the children and women; what did the civilians do?"

More deaths, not on the battlefield, had begun to happen with rapidity. Some resulted from the frequent operations of the federal troops who had taken over the locality.

Common to hear, "three young men shot and killed in Ama Ogudu by people suspected to be Federal troops" or that "Shelling fell and buried a compound in Alayi." It was almost a daily occurrence.

"My mind was getting asphyxiated, not sure I could still think well; more conscious of death, destructions and trying to make meaning out of them all."

"People had all become more religious, hoping on God, sought how He might help. Praying and call for prayers were commonplace."

One of those days Emeuwa heard some people pray – "Oh God, if you spare my life, I'll serve you forever; if you spare my son in the Biafran Army, I'll build you a church… so much of such vows!"

He didn't quite understand all of those; how they prayed so intensely. "I resigned to death like many; didn't see how we're going to survive daily atrocious happenings."

Soon, he joined the prayer bands to pray.

"Oh Lord, please spare my life but if I have to die, let the killers do it when I'm asleep."

Recently, he witnessed the killing of some people by the federal troops. The way one of them struggled after some bullets were pumped into his fragile body; he agonized, cried and fell with blood splattered all over. "Every now and then, I remember it," Emeuwa said.

For the days Emeuwa and family were in the land of the living, what to eat was still a challenge, one as strong as the need for safety, and protection from death.

The farms couldn't produce enough okro for soup; they went for tender cocoa fruits as an alternative. Somebody had suggested that to his Mama. His mother always relied on him to hunt for such necessities.

"Went to the Cocoa farms in Agbonta, downtown settlement with a few other children to harvest them; repeatedly without inhibition or harassment."

The large farm hidden from the public had plenty of cocoa fruits. The trees grew luxuriant but to no use. The farmers couldn't find an alternative market for the seeds.

"We played in the vast space, leaked the ripe before harvesting the fresh tender fruits."

The Plantation owners might've overlooked their naughtiness to help the needy.

As the days so were the gritting and grappling to get supplies for very scarce staple food like yam, cocoyam and hurriedly prepared garri. But the greatest lack was protein-rich food and salt, and others needed to boost immunity and help body cell integrity. It could have been some of the reasons many children fell to Kwashiokor ailment.

"Somebody had come over to tell Papa that people now ate lizards to augment protein needs. Some species of snakes and rats were already accepted as a delicacy."

These animals were untouchable before the war, not part of his people's menu. They were a taboo especially the lizards. In a few days, nobody could see the lizards in their *imeezi* though they bred everywhere. Children hunted them like there was no tomorrow. They made quite some bunch of Biafran pounds from sales; prices were graded depending on size and looks of maturity. The male lizard with a red colour ring around its neck was sold at the highest price.

"Soon a senior friend well-disposed to my playgroup organized us into a hunting gang to go after rats in the bushes and grass cutters."

Emeuwa and his group who returned from the cities were behind in the skills and looked fragile for the hunting expeditions. But some of them desired to be part of the party.

"Was a happy learner, like others; got on with them to move in the bushes, endured the scratches, insect bites, choking thistles that needled my body repeatedly..."

Every catch was celebrated not just among the "hunters" but in the kindred compound because some protein supply was assured. Much effort was made to distribute portions to members of the team and families.

One of the days, the team leader, reputed to be well experienced found a suspected tunnel of a bush rat, *ewi* and was so convinced his team would make a big catch.

He got the team members to make a bonfire at the various points adjudged to be escape routes and began to dig. Half the way, what showed up was a big mole viper.

"I ran for dear life, like others, helter-skelter, especially those of us amateur hunters."

The more experienced found a way to kill the hapless snake. It was big meat worthy of celebration. However, the team wasn't always successful.

Any time they had an off day everybody looked forlorn and carried a long face. The hunters would slip back into their huts, one by one unannounced.

Hard pressed, most people fought back the temptation to violate age-long customs and taboos. Fishing in marine rich *Okpokwuru* stream, very close to the *ezi*, kindred settlement of Emeuwa's family was prohibited.

Okpokwuru was the main source of water for the kindred and a number of surrounding ones.

The very large population of fishes, crabs among other aquatic beings in it heightened the temptation. Often, they danced around the legs of the natives inside the water and at the banks, swimming or scurrying away. Nobody dared touch them.

When some of them died, and floated to the banks, it was a great reminder of the delicacies the natives couldn't have; sumptuous meals they never had in the face of extreme hunger and protein need.

"Kept wondering why we can't eat the fishes, but the refugees quartered in our community feasted on them especially the dead ones."

Older natives always provided so many reasons not to pursue the inquiry. A middle-aged Auntie said "Mgborie went blind because she ate fish from *Okpokwuru*; anybody who fished there would have his or her home filled with overflowing water from *Okpokwuru.*"

Most children seemed to have known about the fable and would often repeat it so much that the scare grew.

"Why hasn't the deity of *Okpokwuru* struck those hunger-ravished refugees who eat them?" Emeuwa asked.

"Seen them a number of times comb the banks of the long-stretched stream hemmed both sides by wild palm plantation, picking fishes, crabs and others."

"None has gone blind; their temporary abodes yet not drowned in water. They're going about normal; desperate for food to survive this starvation Biafran war has brought on all."

"They've guts to hunt in the deity forest, *Afor*, where they throw away people killed by the gods; pick fat snails, harvest luxuriant vegetables of *okazi* and others," Emeuwa added.

Every day, he and playmates and a few others watched out to see what could happen until the refugees left our community to another refugee camp.

At Amauzu, Emeuwa's maternal home kindred, the story was that the refugees did enter the great *Ofia Nsi*, a forbidden place. The thick forest though close to the residential area had been preserved for years for deities few knew anything about. There was a rain forest of luxuriant Iroko trees among others so patterned to allow so much space for a walk.

Some of the green leaves; the size of an umbrella shaded and cooled the park. So pleasant an environment the refugees found shelter, peace walking and relaxing in there.

"The gods don't recognize them, being non-natives," some elders argued.

When more of the refugees left Amaeke Item community, Emeuwa didn't know but only took notice that they weren't milling around any longer.

One day, a folk in the hunting team Emeuwa had joined brought an idea for resolving the dilemma in fishing in *Okpokwuru* stream.

"We fish at the confluence of *Okpokwuru and Ora nnu* streams; that way nobody will accuse us of violating the river deity,"

"Eeeh, how can that be?" Emeuwa and his friends asked.

"At the confluence, the water has no name. Which name will you call it?" Onyeike said.

Onyeike as they knew him, had suggested that at the "confluence of the two streams, those big fishes would cross over from *Okpokwuru* to our fishing tackles; that way the fish can't be said to belong to the fishing-forbidden waters…"

"We will try it…" majority of them chorused.

Farther down the river and far into the farmlands, the two rivers met creating a large body of water which rose and fell at the same time. The streams continued in different courses through the various parts of the farm belt.

So eager they had become to implement the idea without any consultations with parents and the elderly.

"In no time, I made regular catches, some big, others not so big. Mama kept wondering how I brought home fishes everybody was looking for."

Away from fishing, Emeuwa had found another source of protein at the shrine of *Afa Amagbala*, right at the entrance to his kindred compound. Some natives were still bringing fowls for sacrifice to the deity in the marked area covered by raffia palms, leaves and enclosing the main shrine.

He and a few others had tactically assumed the role of attendants at the shrine and were available to deal with the birds offered as sacrifice.

They must be brought alive to the priest who would, after supplications, order that the heads be yanked off to appease the deity. Each of those present at the shrine shared in eating the pepper soup made from the dismembered chicken; cooked without washing.

The pepper soup was eaten with Newbouldia Laevis leaves, *Ogirishi*, weaved into a spoon shape and tacked with broom sticks. Emeuwa found a way to spare some, to bring them home until his father found out.

The angry man caned his son many times for hobnobbing with the others at the shrine. Okocha didn't like that his son was partaking in the rituals. So surprising it was that Okocha took that stance as Ugorji his father, Emeuwa's grandfather was a Priest of the deity, *Afa Amagbala*, well before Emeuwa was born. The protein supply from the shrine ended.

Chapter Seven

Nnanna Nkuma, reputed to be one of the surviving warriors of the inter-village wars visited Papa Emeuwa as he and a few others often did. That is if Okocha wasn't the one visiting.

They often met to compare notes as it were, cry on each other's shoulder and try to relieve the common burden of the ravaging war. Okocha's home was a meeting point of sorts for his role in the 29 Committee and other leadership fora of the village.

They had broken the native Kola nuts without the usual ceremonials and got talking about the latest bombardments that lasted more than 12 hours, from about 8.00pm till about 8.30am.

"So much different from past wars and crises," Grandpa Nkuma said.

"So evident; any comparisons with those wars...? You are the ones who know the history of the past wars," Okocha suggested.

"Those days, the hills and valleys served us some advantage during fighting; things have changed," the old man said.

"Yea, *Nnayi*, you are right. There's so much difference compared to what now is. Can anybody claim to know anything about this war?" Papa Emeuwa asked.

The undulating landscape of Amaeke Item sculptured in the days of inter-village wars hadn't given it any advantage. Those kindred settlements that lay in deep valleys, high hills or behind the cave-like rocks were just there as relics of history.

The long-range shelling machine guns, Jet fighters and bombers were hitting them left, right and centre. Not just Amaeke, all the other eight villages that make up Item, had been targets of the federal troops as often as the troops considered necessary. Their common claim was that they were targeting pockets of Biafran soldiers hiding in the communities.

"Nobody can claim to know all the damages or killings. We've resigned to death of any kind; can you count the number of the dead?" Okocha lamented.

"These days, sound of gun battles from the various war fronts are so close to Amaeke. We are in the middle of it all, I think."

It had begun to look like very little differentiated the war front from the rear.

"So close to our squeezed corners, we are boxed in."

Okom Agbai, Emeuwa's uncle, an ex-Biafran soldier who had joined the discussion asked, "Is there any more difference from the various fronts? There's none...!

"It's on everybody now; you can't tell the deaf that there is commotion in the market," Ete Uka, who had come with Nnanna, a veteran of the World War 11 said.

He had been telling stories of that war and had begun to advocate a community adjustment as most indigenes acknowledge that the federal troops were gradually but firmly taking over every corner of Item town.

Last night as they were about to go to bed it started - persistent gunshots, shelling and all sorts from that time till daybreak.

After a bit of respite, the gun battle resumed. They had packed their pieces of baggage to begin a journey to nowhere in particular.

"Papa and Mama didn't care or say so much as to where to run to, just an escape to an assumed safe place," Emeuwa said.

Luckily, they didn't have to take off that day. It could be another day.

Because of the frequency of the battles, most people were able to capture the "deadly rhythmic" pattern of the sound of the gun shots and ammunitions in their types.

It was them who created lyrical lines - "*kwapu, kwapu, unu dum, kwapu, kwapu, unu dum,* literally meaning pack and run away, pack and run away, all of you."

Those lines aptly mimicked the sound of infantry gun shots accompanied by shelling bombs, hurried and desperate evacuation from settlements any time there was a military action or battle nearby. When often the people fled, nothing mattered except the safety of life. That many missed company and locations of family members, children and parents weren't news any longer. They might reunite or not.

Somehow, Okom Agbai and Okom Jeremiah, both younger brothers of Okocha had learnt to differentiate between the sounds of Biafran guns and those of the Nigerian federal troops. How often they got it right!

That helped to signal when to flee from the settlement into the bush, to stay put or to yield to death. You could hear somebody talk about how he wished to die.

"Better to die where they can gather my corpse and bury me, not a place nobody knows me," some wished.

A week ago in one fleeing instance, some children slipped from the grips of guardians and plunged into the rushing *Okpokwuru* stream.

They were trying to cross to a safer place using the makeshift foot bridge, locally known as *Ogwoh*. And that was from a height of about seven feet above the current water level.

The narrow-improvised foot bridge was made to give room to the rise of the water volume level during the rains.

Made of a big log, cut and placed by young men of the community and laid across the stream, it could only allow one or two persons convenient passage at a time.

Shortly, guardians of the kids who fell into the stream jumped in search of the little ones. Nobody waited to see what happened. Yet as the people fled that day, tens of people struggled to use the bridge all at the same time, adults and children alike.

"With one hand they held each other, with the other on the feeble rail as they counted their steps hoping not to fall into the stream..."

Even with two persons on the foot bridge, you needed some skills to maintain balance on it. How the children laboured to get a grip of the improvised railings!

Yet another night, it should be late 1968 or early 1969, there was such an avalanche of shooting and shelling. The guess was that it must be happening very close, maybe in Abariba, Igbere or other neighbouring towns to Item settlement. Right on, it was Abiriba. Other days it was around Alayi, Ugwueke, or some parts of Nkporo. For a stretch of five days, it happened day and night.

The firing and shelling soon became a pointer to the displacement of Emeuwa's family and other indigenes of the Amaeke Item community.

Towards the end of that week, Emeuwa's parents had responded to a certain session of gun fire and shelling and got the family to flee. As usual, nobody was certain where to.

Interior forest or...? There they lived in the bush for about a week or so.

The "run" must have been caused by the last battle between federal and Biafran troops around Abiriba after which federal troops took absolute control of the remaining communities of the Bende division or so it looked.

"We returned to our family house for some days," Emeuwa said.

But as the "scampering, *osondu*" became frequent Mama Emeuwa had an idea of how to prepare her children to live as refugees. And to cut down on the number of pieces of baggage she struggled to carry during those escapes.

"Day and night you must wear at least three clothes, especially when going to bed," Mama commanded. It must be adhered to strictly unless you want some beating at your bare back, upper part of the body..."

"Never will you know when it'll happen; with extra clothes, you've something to wear for some time as a refugee," Mama Emeuwa argued.

Emeuwa's often complaints didn't change anything; his Mama wouldn't listen. Repeatedly she told him, "*Mechionu, keep quiet,* what do you even know?"

"Me, Iroanya Charity and Onu wore three clothes to sleep at night from hence," Emeuwa said.

Chapter Eight

Emeuwa and his Papa took two turns to the right to join the path between a stretch of thick forest and wild fallow farms. It was their way going back home to Amaeke Item, about five kilometres away.
They were coming from Nkporo and would first get to Apanu Item. From Apanu it was a straight road to Amaeke.
Apanu, the source community of the whole of Item town is bounded from that angle by a clan of Nkporo town, where father and son had gone to do business.
From Apanu Item on the straight-line connection, you would access Amaeke, then Amaokwe and Okoko. Unlike the other five communities of Item scattered out like branches – Akanu, Umuaekpa, Amaekpu, Okagwe, and Okai. All nine made up Item town.
Nkporo, further down the east of Item was a largely agrarian community, slightly different from Item, but shared some cultural similarities. Not too far from Afikpo and could be accessed through Edda and Akaeze communities away from Item.
That day, the two left Nkporo a little earlier through the only road in use after finishing with buying and selling tubers of yam.
They had got wind of the rumours of some untoward activities on the road and how it was increasingly becoming lonely to walk. But many hadn't stopped using it inspite of those reports.
"They aren't as much as on other roads," some of the natives claimed. "It's really the only one of its kind that leads to Apanu straight on…"

"Yes, not as busy; travellers meet one or two persons in a long while."

"No motor vehicles. How many are available? We don't see them anymore use the road," one of the natives and a customer of Papa Emeuwa had said. "Only those military motors I see.'

Trekking on the sharp gravel-filled red soil was the only option and often done bare-foot. Shoes had worn out and couldn't be replaced.

Emeuwa and father had walked for about 45 minutes when they sighted a lone, kitted soldier, something considered to be a bad omen in 1969.

Soon, Mazi Amadu Okocha had begun to mutter words his son couldn't immediately understand. Emeuwa said he could only pick "tell them what happened to me." The second time Mazi said that he was shivering.

Emeuwa was quick to ask, "Papa, tell them what…?"

"Can't you see?" Okocha shouted at the son.

"Will he shoot us…?" Emeuwa asked

"Tell them; tell them… *mechieonu! Keep quiet.*"

The kitted soldier marching towards them was now less than 100 metres away. The winding bush path they walked could only reveal the soldier's full stature when he got that close.

"What would the soldier do now or not?" Mazi Okocha tried to resolve as he continued to hold on to Emeuwa. He had started slowing down, stopping moment by moment. All his mind could fathom was that he and his son were the only ones in the vicinity. Everywhere was calm.

"Anything could happen without interruptions or even records"! He thought. "Nobody is coming or going on this road. Nothing happening in the bush I'm looking at."

The nearest village, Apuanu was still more than one kilometer away from where they met the soldier.

"Could this be it, my final day in this war? This soldier is well prepared, can shoot, kill here very fast."

Based on past experiences Okocha feared what could happen and whether he would be as lucky as he had been in the time past. The soldier appeared ready for anything, his menacing visage and kitting bore witness.

His uniform clearly showed he was one of the Nigerian Federal soldiers. There was no Biafran sun anywhere on it. Biafran soldiers didn't kit that way.

"He kept marching steadily towards us in his might almost oblivious of two of us," Okocha added.

It could've been in August of that year when the war seemed to have gone out of control, perhaps the most traumatic belt.

Everybody had become aware that one-on-one encounter on a lonely road with a soldier could lead to instant death. There had been reports of such occurrences in other parts of Item and neighbouring towns.

"So quickly told Emeuwa all; the only one with me; to tell the story of how I was killed."

Mazi Okocha couldn't imagine his boy might suffer the same fate. "…small boy, I must be the target…."

Emeuwa gazed at his flustered Papa, said "*Chineke Ekwola*, God forbid. Papa, let's run, let's run…"

"Nooooo; no, he will shoot quickly."

"*Welu*, what else…? Upon all these struggles to cater for the family; *tachio obu*, let them know; I've tried," Okocha deposed.

It wasn't the first time Father and son went to Nkporo and returned from the popular yam market though it was a journey of about five kilometers.

Trading in farm products was one of the businesses Okocha resorted to in the absence of his normal one just to cater for his large family of 12.

"I must continue to try until life is no more", he often said to his family before going on any of such journeys.

A younger relative, Ottah Ottah had suggested he slowed down citing increased risks in movements.

"Anybody, at this time, no matter the age could be killed on suspicion or in anticipatory self-defence," Ottah had said a few days ago.

At almost ten now, Emeuwa had become his permanent escort, better, a partner since the older son couldn't afford to show up for the risk of being conscripted into the Biafran army. Or even shot at by the federal soldiers on the suspicion of being a disguised member of Biafran Organization of Freedom Fighters, BOFF.

Of all the places in the part of Bende, Nkporo further down the north of the Division was renowned for growing large tubers of yam. For the large productions, the tubers of yam sold cheap. It was the Mecca for low-priced farm produce especially yam.

Amadu Okocha wouldn't do the alternative *Afia Attack*, the more lucrative but dangerous night trading across military posts of both the federal and the Biafran soldiers because of distance and the high risks.

The Nkporo market was a pleasant alternative being adjudged calmer and safer by all assumptions and was the hometown of some of Mazi's former business associates. He had discussed his decision for the Nkporo market with his family which included three wives. Starvation was intensifying and everybody was trying his or her hands at something to earn a living.

"Need to do this… a little is better…" he often told his wives and children.

For all the trips to and from Nkporo in the last three months, he never experienced any danger until that fateful day. He had some other times but on different turfs.

"I cheated death when I dodged arrest of federal soldiers who stormed to take leaders of the *29 Committee* on account of squealed info," Amadu said.

Between April and May 1968, Okocha had also escaped being conscripted into the Biafran Armed Forces. In his 50s, he looked very much younger because of his fitness and smart appearance. What gave him recognition with women and men almost got him into the "trouble" of becoming a reluctant Biafran soldier.

"They came totting their Madison rifles, hurled young men into waiting pick-up vehicles. Know what? Jumped fence, meandered through *azu oka* to *iyi Okpokwuru* bordering our compound," he said.

The third time he escaped life-endangering situation was early in 1969. The bullets of the federal troops who came on a sting operation narrowly missed his head and chopped off a portion of his right ear. The scar remained unmistakable.

A member of the 29 Committee, Sam Anya had turned S*abo*, the Biafran lingo for the saboteur, and leaked information on the inner workings of the Committee. Luckily, some of the key members escaped including Mazi Okocha, OGB Maduka, and another of the prominent leaders of the committee. Thereafter, they operated undercover.

So, Mazi Okocha went about believing that death stalked him, maybe more than it did other civilians as the war raged. At such times, he was quick to verbalize his will to any relative around. When he sighted that soldier on their way from Nkporo, it didn't matter whether he was Biafran or Nigerian.

"A chanced meeting with a straggler of a soldier is the closest face to face encounter, I recall," Okocha said.

"To run as usual or duck, leave my poor son behind. I couldn't make that decision. Thought also of confronting the soldier as he appeared alone but…?" Okocha began to take notice that the federal soldier was missing his steps as he got closer to them.

"Could've been the weight of his ammunitions," he thought as he tried to guess what the matter could be. And where the soldier could be coming from?

"Why's he alone or are others coming behind?"

From some 100 meters away, he couldn't gauge those staggering steps of the soldier except that he wore a camouflage uniform, bullet-proof helmet, strapped rifle fitted with bayonet, black boot to fit and those other tuck-ins like water bottle, bullets bag etc. He looked like one going to execute an operation. Mazi didn't stop talking to his boy, Emeuwa, "tell them what happened to me. May God keep you all…!"

"It's over, you can see; *meta obughu ike, inula*. Take heart ehn, take heart."

As they got much closer, a few meters from the soldier, Amadu bursted out, "Good afternoon, sir, good afternoon, sir, afternoon sir" in that hurried sequence. But the soldier wouldn't respond.

Rather, "he bumped into us, don't know; can't say what happened thereafter," Okocha indicated.

"On my back at the ground, saw that Emeuwa had fallen the other way into a fallow farm, side of the bush path."

"Thanks sir, thanks sir, don't mind the stupid boy," Mazi said repeatedly lying on his back on the ground. The soldier didn't stop, kept moving away from Okocha and the son.

They laid on the ground awhile; the soldier continued on his way. On their feet now but still dazed; Papa and son couldn't make any movement, only darted their eyes various directions.

The soldier was steadily heading to Nkporo out of the immediate sight of the two journey persons. A section of the bush blurred their sight of him as he moved on. But Okocha and son could still trace his motion with the scrapping of his boots and swerving of grown weeds to his body's movement.

"Was it well with the soldier, drunk or what"? Okocha was still checking as they began to recover.

The Nigerian soldier never had time to look at Okocha or ask their normal question — *"wetin da reason*? "What is it?"

Soldiers of the federal troops were known to patronize lots of palm wine and gin bars in Apuanu, the village from where the soldier was coming.

"He might've been one of those who go there to eat specially prepared 'bush' meat from undomesticated animals and was returning to base," Okocha guessed.

As they gathered themselves, they first ran farther into the bush.

"We're falling into ditches, crawling out, until we lost all the strength" Amadu Okocha said.

They began to move towards the path step by step, trying to catch some breath, closer to the path, peeping and checking the road if there were other soldiers on sight.

When they couldn't sight the soldier or any other, they returned to the path, increased pace, walked and ran at the same time.

From that distance, they felt assured that the soldier must surely be walking towards Nkporo. Amadu Okocha and the son faced up towards Apuanu, the village next to his home.

As they got to the centre of Apuanu village, a distance of about one and a half Kilometres from the scene of the incident, Mazi turned to his son, Emeuwa, *"ekele duru Obasi d'relu.* Hmmm, thank God who is in Heaven," he hissed.

"But let's move faster, faster…" as if the soldier was going to return for them. Emeuwa panted, laboured to match the increased pace of his father as usual.

They both got home panting, but it didn't matter. Mazi Okocha had escaped "certain" death again, the fourth time, or so he thought.

He was the one who told the story. All of his family members, he had assembled, as many as were home.

"Kele nu Obasi d'relu, thank God in Heaven; I was dead, really. *Soja Nde Igaba* almost killed me… God didn't allow it."

In the next two months, Mazi Okocha wouldn't go to Nkporo. He re-routed to Amaekpu, a community of Item, some two and a half kilometers from Amaeke.

The people had a way with farming too including yams. But Amaekpu wasn't as big a market as Nkporo.

Chapter Nine

Their bodies bore the lacerations of the war: extreme emaciation and faded and rumpled clothes, injuries and then, forlon postures -. adults and children. But Papa Emeuwa hadn't relented to lead them along arduous paths, to trudge on inspite of their sorry state. They were of the few families to arrive the barn early from interior bush they had been hiding in. Okocha, family and other relatives were returning home. They had been running and hiding inside the bush for the days of operations of the Nigerian army in Amaeke.

He had led them this far towards home. It was just moments ago that they got to the community yam barn in the midst of a massive orchard. Somebody had suggested that they should wait. Parents and elders were consulting. But the children had started to wail for food; nobody was sure where it would come from. Something must be done. Everybody seemed to be looking in the direction of Grand Mama Ulo Elu Onyeaku. The portion of the barn they were in was hers. She inherited it from her late husband, Ugorji Iko. It looked like she had accepted responsibility. She did her "magic" to provide a bowl of roasted yam; it had been set before the children after many hours. "Clean your eyes, it's okay; you can stop sobbing," one of the parents consoled the children, all grandchildren of Grandma.

The big heap of roasted yam cut into small pieces and stewed in palm oil and ground pepper was it. The eating was another battle. You must gear up before another took your portion. Every group eating had been like that.

Whining and complaints were competing with hunger at the same time. Grandma Ulo Elu Onye Aku approached the section the crowd of her grandchildren gathered for the eating.

Omeoga and his "gang" didn't like that she had appeared to intervene. They didn't at all. Her emergence had diffused their tricks to get more share of the insufficient food at the expense of their younger siblings.

"Who invited Nnenne? Omeoga had queried in a low tone.

"Should she be looking for whom to hit with her walking stick?" He grumbled. The cries of the vulnerable younger ones had reached her ears.

Omeoga, the eldest at 14 and twelve others in the age range of six to 10 made up the crowd. They had been starving for nearly two days. Along with their parents, had been running from shelling bombs and aerial bombardments on their Amaeke Item homestead. The Nigerian federal troops had carried a battle to Biafran soldiers allegedly hiding in the community.

For that number of days, without food, they dared to eat anything that could quench their hunger. All the wild fruits they ate couldn't fill their starving stomach.

Everyone was on *osondu, safety stampede* — from home to the bush and from the bush to their partly damaged homes.

Okocha and his relatives were saying that the incident was one of the unforgettable episodes in the middle of 1969; of the Nigeria-Biafra war of atrocities. If the war was coming to an end, it wasn't so known by the people and the federal soldiers didn't act it. It was still war, a war in this part of the theatre.

After three and half days of hiding and groping in the thick rain forests, swamps and gullies, they were a bit relieved that they had started towards home though hungry. Some people were affirming that the coast was clear. The federal troops who mounted at key parts of the community — the hills and the valleys had begun to withdraw, retreating to Umunnato Military camp, about five kilometres away or more from Amaeke.

At the barn, the return journey, they had covered nearly eight kilometres on foot and had agreed to stop over there, a large section reserved for the storage and preservation of yams and seedlings. It mirrored the wealth of the average and rich yam farmers.

Though it was hidden from the public it hadn't been spared totally of damages. It retained its manicured pavements and large trees that helped to shield it from the prying eyes of invading soldiers. But those running through it had damaged lots of the yam tubers. From the location to the residential areas was nearly one kilometre.

"We've got to wait for the report of the spies," Papa Emeuwa had earlier indicated.

The spies, young men, some ex-Biafran recruits, had gone to re-confirm the situation going through the banks of the *Okpokwuru* stream. But the grandchildren who cried earlier were of the few who still had small strength to signal their bad hungry situation. At the eastern part of the barn, coming out from the bush, a collection of about 20 children in groups wailed; on the opposite side, some laid on the ground as if they had fainted. Food of any kind would help but all that appeared to be available at the barn were trampled pulp of yam plastering the floor.

"Nothing else..." the women had lamented.

Grand Mama, Uloelu, aged about 80 who saved the day as usual was able to get some tubers of yam that escaped the destruction; four of them so hidden away.

Quickly, she had guided Omeoga to climb and reach his hands into corners of the strands of the layers of the barn to bring them down. No other person could've seen those tubers. Omeoga beamed with smiles after touching the yams and took them out one after the other.
"There's still more Nnenne," he said.
"*Mechionu*, come down, *ngwangwa*, Nnenne answered. Some had started to beam smiles as they watched the act.
"*Haaa*, Nnenne, how did you do this? *Nnem a sirike, this grandmama is strong,*" they seemed to chorus.
Bonfire was made from dried leaves and tree branches fetched from nearby fallow farms to roast the four big tubers. Only God knew from where she got palm oil and some ground red pepper. Some of the daughters-in-law were now helping. The food was ready. The children had the first go before any other.
All of the 13 children were gulping and chewing fast the roasted yam but Omeoga and two others older, about 11years old wanted to secure a greater portion for themselves citing their seniority in age.
"Dee Orji Omeoga, this won't be enough for us," the younger siblings begged, and cried. Others had started to complain. Everybody wanted more, the food they hadn't eaten in more than 48 hours.
Emeuwa was one of those who instigated the inivation of Nnenne. Agwu Wems had sneaked out to inform Grand Mama, Uloelu. Before Omeoga and company could do much, Grand Mama arrived with her bent and dried, rugged walking stick she slightly leaned on.
"Leave everything in the bowl, no special portions; bring those ones back. Don't hide anything," she thundered.
"No, no special treatment, everybody is hungry. When it comes to food, nobody is king. They've never used the size of appetite or 'stomach' to determine who should be

a leader," Grand Mama said popping her sunken scary eyes. She gazed intently at Omeoga Orji.

The younger ones shouted in unison, *"ezi Nnenne, me-kaa."*

With some wry smiles and relief, they proceeded to gulp the roasted yam at a normal pace as much as their small mouths could take. Omeoga and his "clique" faced down and ate. Nobody could dare the vehemence of the very stern grandmama. "They feared and respected her" not only for her age. She was revered as a leader of women and one who could stand side by side with men.

Chapter Ten

The fear of being bombed at the market wasn't as strong as it was before. So, they headed to *Afia Eke*, the main market of Amaeke, located more or less at the centre of the community. It was Eke ukwu, the prime market day. Being in the market that day fairly guaranteed some transactions. It normally attracted the biggest crowd of buyers and sellers. The sellers came in batches carrying all sorts of vegetables, condiments, yam tubers, cocoyam and others; sellers and buyers who desired to have a better bargain made it to the market.

Afia Eke at Nde Okoroha was the only place reserved by the community leadership for such large number of sellers and buyers though some sell their wares in smaller kindred demarcations. But it won't be *Afia Eke*.

Emeuwa and his Mama had trekked about a quarter of a kilometre from their Eziufu settlement to the market. As at 11am they arrived; that should be almost one hour before the ultimate start time. Their wares: pieces of African star apple and *Oha* soup making vegetable they hoped to exchange for Biafran Pounds.

Quickly, mother and son claimed and occupied a spot for the sales; no shade over it like all others though most traders used their torn and worn-out umbrellas or broad cocoyam leaves as shield from the sun. There were no formal allocations of the spots; ownership and occupation were temporary, only valid for the day. The first seller to arrive on the spot had possession.

For part of their wares, Emeuwa had climbed one of the tallest *Oha* bearing trees, about 22 feet, in his kindred compound to get the skye-green vegetable. The climb, bare-hand gripping and twisting of the legs across the slippery, fat, smooth stem of the tree. Gradually and steadily, he scaled up near the tips of the branches bearing the *Oha* vegetables. Ownership of the trees had long ancestry and passed from generation to generation.

Emeuwa had followed and quickly learnt to climb since he returned with his family from Aba in 1968 and had added the early morning runs for *Udara* to his repertoire of entreprenuerial skills. Not many children who were born in the cities, so learnt. He was beginning to look enabled to help to solve the hunger and lacks facing his family like other children were doing.

Settled at a corner facing the main road, he and mother had hurriedly claimed, they displayed the vegetables and pieces of *Udara*. It was time to canvass for buyers as they weren't the only sellers of *Oha* and *Udara* that day.

Shortly, Emeuwa crossed over the un-tarred main road to invite a prospective buyer and was talking with her when a detachment of Nigerian federal soldiers drove in, in their trucks. Everyone began to shake, fidget, then some murmurs and movment backwards. He and prospect discontinued the market talk as the lady disappeared into the nearby kindred compound with such a speed. The soldiers had arrived in their usual bravado though they didn't look in their direction.

"It must be for the usual; hunting expedition or arrest of suspected offenders..." one of those standing close to Emeuwa whispered.

Kitted to the hilt, ammunitions hanging on their necks and shoulders like garlands, the sight of them and brisk movements alarmed the people. It must be an intentional show of superiority or conquest over the people and territory, some indigenes judged.

The soldiers brandished their long, black rifles to complement their arsenal of intimidation. Those would be enough to further cow the on-looking villagers, or to abduct any woman for a wife, partner or something. Once in their grip, no lady could be rescued even by the most jealous and bravest of a husband.

The two patrol trucks headed further down to the other end of the village market, perhaps to choose a vantage point for the start of the operations.

Hardly had they advanced further from *Afia Eke* that they caught up with Lizzy Erinma jiggling home on the other side of the road.

"*Kai, kwom here amariya,*" one of them thundered.

"*Kwom here…*" he commanded again, raising his long black shinning rifle.

Lizzy didn't think the soldier was talking to her and continued; her pace increased just quickly. It wasn't up to five minutes that she left the market, trudging home with soup condiments she had bought for a relative.

"*Kpuo kpuo, Kpuo kpuo…*" a Sergeant and another jumped from the vehicle hitting the ground with such bounce that confirmed their soldierly fitness. It was the Sergeant, who went across the road grinning, firm-gripped Lizzy's tender right hand, and gently dragged her towards their truck.

"*Hafum aka, hafum aka…*" she cried, twisting, wriggling to lose her tiny hand from the grip of the firm assailant, a soldier who could be about 30 years old or more. Before anybody could ask what was happening, the soldier goaded her into the carrier of their vehicle to join three other women whose clothes were already soaked in their tears.

The Sergeant went to the front cabin of the truck and whispered something to one who looked like an Officer, perhaps the leader of the detachment before the truck moved again and followed by the other one.

Observing villagers moved as fast as they could out of the sight of the soldiers. They could be suspecting what would happen next. Nobody was sure. From their hiding places inside their huts near the road, they watched as the military vehicles swerved and moved on.

Those who could challenge the abduction or plead for the little girl were gone, in hiding. Would they come from there to help? The captured, poor Lizzy and company wouldn't do anything to free themselves from those fierce-looking soldiers determined to have their way!

They didn't have any weapons; the soldiers had all of those.

"Perhaps, only those who could challenge death as they say or had sworn to go to the land of the spirits would try."

When they took Lizzy into their truck, Emeuwa was said to have followed closely out of their immediate sight, taking some paths not so well known to non-natives.

The prospecting soldier discussed further with the leader of the detachment, returned and said something that suggested they would go to Lizzy's home.

Lizzy was said to have resigned to fate on hearing that. She cried a bucket full, soaking her clothes - the only thing she and the other victims could do.

Looking at the women already in the vehicle in their languid and teary state gave her the clearest indications of a bad omen.

"Could this lead to death or what…?" Lizzy tried to reason, fully reminiscent that a number of men and women the federal soldiers took away earlier were yet to return. The federal soldiers were nobody's friend except their drinking pals and those who pimped for them.

Now the prospective husband with her at the back carrier of the truck was busy asking, *"wetin da reason"* while tears poured from her eyes. Other soldiers looked on amused or less concerned. They might have their own time another day.

"When they said to me, *your Papa, gwo see* I almost passed out not knowing what it could mean," Lizzy was reported to have said.

But the Sergeant kept saying *"me, husband, you wife, hahahurhur, amariya,"* she told later. She had mindlessly pointed down the road to her kindred settlement, *Agbonta,* Amaeke Item, the same way to the home of Eze Ogo, the village head.

It was the fifth time in the month of February 1969 that the soldiers were in Amaeke to "hunt" for female partners.

Young women or wives who strayed to their path or ran out of luck from their hiding were the usual targets. Girls of the age of Lizzy weren't until that day.

The military trucks kept moving in the direction Lizzy pointed to. Before they got to *Agbonta,* her kindred people had deserted their homes. It was said that as soon as the residents got wind of what was happening, they hastened to the nearby bushes, orchards and *obandi,* yam barn. Lizzy's parents had joined the fleeing horde.

Inside the kindred compound, they turned left and entered the next house with a courtyard decorated with native chalk, kaolin and *uri,* local decor black paint. It was the *Obu* of the Eze Ogo, Chief Onyeike, aged about 78 years.

On the way, the soldiers took along *Seriki,* their appointed Regent, who normally translated their message from Hausa or Yoruba to Igbo language. After some exchanges at the *Obu,* an announcement came, "Lizzy has been married to Staff Sergeant Aminu Uba," Seriki reported in Igbo language to the hearing of the Eze Ogo. The village head sighed, faced down, looked up and suggested that they might need an older girl, but the new husband was motioning with his hands and shouting, *"Walahi... No..."*

"I've heard. *Obughu bu nna nwanta*, I'm not the father. How else should I answer *nde agha soja*?" Eze Ogo said further.

Some of the soldiers stood as they discussed with Eze Ogo and Seriki while a number of them outside took combatant positions. In a few minutes, they stormed out and jumped into their truck headed out of the compound.

They must have been satisfied with the additional catch that was Lizzy. The three ladies Lizzy joined in the truck could have been from other Item communities. Nobody knew precisely which ones they were.

Through other sections of Amaeke community, the detachment headed towards the next village, Amaokwe Item. Perhaps on their way back to Umunnato Military camp, about five kilometers away. That would be the right place for the soldiers to party for yet another set of new wives, something that had become their past time, villagers believed.

"It's their way of celebrating conquest and, the women as trophies of war," a native had suggested.

Soon, the news of the capture of Lizzy spread to the whole community. Everyone talked about how she was the youngest ever of the numerous women taken by the soldiers.

"How will this small girl cope...?" Most parents queried as often as they could discuss the Lizzy matter.

Even if the questions were rhetoric, those parents only raised them behind the earshot of the federal soldiers;

when they had gone back to their barracks, and their informants believed not to be around.

Nde Ada forum, a group of daughters from her kindred, had gathered to discuss the matter. Soon they began to cry at the perceived "wickedness done to their younger mates and now the youngest of all, Lizzy".

"*Okaghu echoru, nwa mpansi,* small innocent girl, she isn't of age yet," they chorused.

Emeuwa had also taken the news to his playmates, loosely known as *Umurima Eziufu*. He told the story mimicking the gestures and stomping of the soldiers and added other snippets he got from other indigenes.

He had hardly completed the story when all of them went into a chorus of wailing, like a rehearsed orchestra. Nobody could console the other. They so cried for about 25 minutes until they were able to regain sobriety. Wiping their eyes, they sat disorderly at the corner behind Obu Eziufu, community hall, where they met often; their heads drooping in apparent hopelessness.

Some were still on the floor when one of them asked, "is this how it's going to be? Will she come back?"

One of them walked out wailing, another followed, and a number of others stood and sauntered away. They went back home wiping their tears. Many of them didn't wait to ask their parents questions to make meaning out of the incident. Emeuwa had asked uncle Agbai. All that he was told, "*Nde Igaba* have married her."

"What's the meaning... how is that a marriage? He asked again.

"Will they do a wedding party? How's Lizzy, now a wife...?"

Emeuwa tried to review the aspects of the drama he witnessed, like a scene in a dream or a movie!

Ogbeyialu, Lizzy's closest friend in the playgroup had asked her own parents, why the soldiers took and called her wife!

"It's a matter of war *nnem*; it wouldn't have happened if not..." they were reported to have told her.

Emeuwa and Agbai got talking again about Lizzy.

"Wasn't she the one playing with you people on those heaps of sand at *Ologho* the other day? Has she even outgrown bathing outside, in the backyard?" Agbai asked.

While Lizzy, Emeuwa and others in *Umurima Eziufu* group played together, they thought nothing about her as the soldiers did. "Perhaps, they hadn't grown eyes to gaze at her protruding small, firm breasts and forming hips," some adults guessed.

None of the kids had taken particular notice of Lizzy's freshly sprouting pubic hairs. Nobody was certain that Lizzy too had understood the incipient puberty changes happening all over her body for that matter.

If she had, she wouldn't be running around with those children on their turf or bath with them beside *azuoka*. They all did when they couldn't go to the *iyi* for a bath. "Why not...? Is any of them older than 11?" One of the parents had said. Only the older people would've made certain about Erinma's burgeoning womanhood! Something the errant and triumphant soldiers wanted desperately. Now they've got it in Lizzy and couldn't wait; they had to, with their guns and jackboots.

"They've taken her innocence, the collective innocence of the children, Uncle Agbai deposed. "Can *Umurima Eziufu* ever behave normal, revel in the innocence that makes them children? I doubt!" He continued. "Yes, like adults, they strive for money, upkeep; do one thing or the other to survive, because of the war but everybody knows that they're still kids, in thought and in deed," he stated.

"Inspite of your strides, you are children; kidding away in the throes of this war" Papa Emeuwa said and smiled.

"We see you as ones who still bathe only your bellies?" The next day Emeuwa was brooding over Lizzy's matter and remembered a discussion his mother had with one of her friends, Mama Ikodiya.

It was at the inner side of their kitchen and a few weeks before the incident.

He wouldn't remember everything about the discussion but about Lizzy Erinma only these aspects. "The girl is a potential great beauty," Mama said.

"I've advised Lizzy's mother to dissuade her from bathing with these children outside; she no longer belonged there. Nobody would have believed that she survived a bout of kwashiokor a few months ago", Mama Emeuwa added. According to them, the forming of her hips was fast for a 12year old. "Looks she'll be the big hips type," Mama Ikodiya reasoned. Mama Emeuwa kept mute awhile. Mama Ikodiya had said she overheard some young men saying, "a little more time, Lizzy's bowlegs, dreamy eyes and luxuriant eyebrows that always looked like it is touched up by eye pencil, will drive men crazy."

Mama Emeuwa added, "...her broad smiles, extravagant greetings... hmmm." She drew Mama Ikodiya to herself. "Let's hope her mother'll do the needful as we've discussed".

Named Elizabeth Erinma Egbuta at birth, she had become popular among her mates with the moniker, Lizzy. To many, that was as much an acceptable stylish anglicization of her name. It sounded as beautiful as her native *Erinma*. The middle name Erinma, many believed, was given at birth in praise of her natural beauty. Many had come to assume it was the Igbo version of Lizzy.

"Learnt that one of the teachers in her primary school and an Amaeke indigene made popular the name, Lizzy," Emeuwa told.

Lizzy was gone and continued to live with the Sergeant in that kind of marriage as the war continued to rage.

The year she was taken, federal troops were said to have taken charge of substantial part of the vast town known traditionally as Item Okpi. It was through a military manoeuvre people expressed as "cut off." They appeared to dominate most of the communities in the belt of Bende Division, according to Agbai.

Agbai said, "cut off" meant that the Nigerian Army went behind the defence of the Biafran soldiers to take those communities."

They had taken over the communities such that the people couldn't connect to other Biafrans easily.

Only surreptitiously could those reach out to other Biafrans in other areas, often at the risk of being shot at by federal troops on the suspicion of being a spy for Biafra.

Now the federal soldiers from time to time visited these "cut-off" communities to pick out "enemies, or fish for booties of war."

Women were an important part of these booties. The enemies, young and middle-aged men suspected to be members of BOFF. Sometimes, it looked like the booties were the stronger attraction.

"Should they also be looking for small girls like Lizzy," some of the people worried.

She had to live with her new soldier "husband" at that tender age!

Some weeks had passed, and Lizzy's parents and relatives desired to go to Umunnato Military Camp to plead for her release; or just to see her.

But nobody had the courage to undertake the journey with them, not knowing how the soldiers would react to the visit.

"Assuming the 'husband' and colleagues get angry at us, misreading it to mean affront…?" Some relatives reasoned.

"Maybe we call Seriki to navigate us to the place," some of them suggested. But Seriki neither accepted nor refused to assist. When he responded, it didn't lead to any visit. Some alleged "he wanted a bribe."

Mr and Mrs Igwo Egbuta neither showed the willingness to nor were they able to provide any material in lieu; they were in the group most hit by lack and war-induced poverty.

Emeuwa had gone on one of his usual errands for his Mama a month or so after the abduction of Lizzy. He wouldn't count the number of times his mother sent him because her health had further deteriorated. Emeuwa was her present help.

He had gone to Amaokwe, the next village on the west of Amaeke which was closer to the federal military command centre and there walked into a group of young people scampering away from the settlement.

They ran so frightfully and alarmed on-lookers. He joined the boys and girls to run. By the manifest vigour with which they ran you could imagine they might also win an Olympic race if they entered for it. But they weren't in any athletic competition.

Away from the settlements, they jumped over ditches, crawled through yawning gullies and barricades; didn't care about skin-tearing thistles all around the places.

They headed to various directions to get away from danger that had been constant. The searched-for-shield was thinning out; only a few places could have been hidden from the prying eyes of the federal troops. In a few minutes, they were in the bush; laid low inside those patches and wild orchards like people dodging bullets.

Emeuwa was in Amokwe to execute his mother's errand to his Aunt Ude and chanced on those young people scampering from the settlement. He had to save his life before doing the errand.

That Mama had spat on the ground, and warned, "Emeuwa, don't let the saliva dry up before you return otherwise your navel will decay," didn't matter anymore to him.

He had run straight to Amokwe in little over 25 minutes, a distance of about one and a half kilometres and met up with those frightful children escaping from federal soldiers.

Emeuwa said he ran with those young people without asking questions because "it is better to run first...."

"Many, who wanted to know what, took bullets or got wounded, labelled, arrested and taken to unpleasant places," a remark often repeated when discussing tactics for dealing with federal soldiers.

Right inside the bush, he gathered himself to find out the reasons. "Aaah, *Nde Igaba* are around ooo," Ogala, a native teenager, had answered.

Igaba, a coded descriptive of the Nigerian fetderal soldiers and the dangers they often delivered to the people: merciless killings of suspected supporters of Biafra, especially those accused of hobnobbing with members of BOFF and the frequent abduction of young women among others.

"They are in pursuit of some young people and have captured two boys and four girls already," Ogala continued.

"They're many oo; saw many of their vehicles driving like they wanted to crash. Yes, some of them were marching on the ground towards *Atanko*…"

"*Chaa* …" one of the boys shouted, sprang up; others joined him to run up farther crossing to a nearby bush on the way to Akanu Item, another of the constituent community of Item.

Emeuwa and those would hibernate in that bush from about 10am till about 3pm when they got some hint the coast might be clear.

Two by two they began to move out, to find their way back to the kindred settlements.

"Missed my way a few times before getting back to Amaeke road at about 3.30pm," Emeuwa said.

Along with a band of men and women heading that way, he went and didn't bother to go see the Auntie his mother had sent him.

Back at Nde Okoroha, the business centre of Amaeke, Emeuwa had learnt that some soldiers were also in Agbonta, Lizzy's kindred settlement. He was encouraged to continue.

As he got to *Ologho Eziufu,* the massive meeting place of the whole of Amaeke which also led to Agbonta, everything was in frenzy. More people walked with such fright that you would think they could disappear from the surface of the earth.

"Some natives around the entrance to the kindred compound darted eyes right, left and centre ran a little to get out of the compound," Emeuwa observed.

The soldiers had accompanied Lizzy to visit with her family for the first time, a little over one month since she was captured and forcefully married. Her husband, the

Sergeant, and a few colleagues marched to Agbonta after alighting from their Land-rover truck parked beside *Ologho Eziufu*. They walked past the *Obu* of the Ezeogo, as Lizzy in front led the way to the home of her parents.

A bit, unlike the soldiers, she walked dragging her fleshier body, resplendent in her "non-Biafran clothes."

"It didn't look like her anymore, now much like somebody older than 12," some people said.

Some of Emeuwa's playmates from Agbonta said that one of the soldiers beckoned on the people running away, smiling broadly. "*Me in-law, baa trouble;* gesticulates with his two hands, his rifle strapped to his back," the soldier was reported to have said repeatedly.

The entourage ended up in Lizzy's family thatch-roofed house built years ago with red mud.

Mr and Mrs Igwo Egbuta had meant to hide like others but changed their mind to receive the visiting soldiers on sighting Lizzy. They had desired to see her.

Lips and limbs trembling intermittently they struggled to welcome the visitors – *Jokwanu, unu abia wo*, they greeted with trembling lips. But the inlaw, struggling to be friendly gestured, smiled broadly and made explanations to calm nerves. Sergeant Aminu, Lizzy's husband speaking in his laboured Pidgin English helped to calm them down.

"*Baa trouble, Walahi,*" the Sergeant said repeatedly.

Off-loading of packages of canned food, rice and others brought inside their house might have helped.

Some of those were dropped on the pavement as the off-loaders couldn't find space in the cramped one-bed room apartment. Pieces of their belongings recovered from their former residence in Aba also littered the apartment.

Seated in the squeezed living room of the Egbutas, were Sergeant Aminu and two of his colleagues. Nobody came near the hut while they were there.

"*My waifu, good, good, baa wahala, trouble...*" Sergeant was said to have told the family. "*Me, do well, baa trouble, ka chi ko...*"

The discussions didn't last up to 10 minutes before they bounced out, walked a bit and boarded the truck that brought them, on their way back to camp. Nobody was taken or shot on that day.

For the two days Lizzy stayed, some natives visited as if they came to pay condolences or to "verify" the state of the family.

A good number would snicker thereafter, "hope all is well, Erinma's looking good ooo... hmmm." That much they could see.

Meanwhile, her mother, it was reported, had confided in some friends that Lizzy behaved like one "uncertain of something."

"Wanted to go see her at their house but my mother wouldn't allow me," Emeuwa said.

"Next time, I tried; Lizzy had gone back to her soldier husband at Umunnato." When he told his mother, Mama Emeuwa retorted that Lizzy had gone to do "*iyakaba* with *Nde Igaba*, prostitution with federal soldiers," and advised him to cut association with her. Lizzy had been grouped along irreverent young women who jumped at providing consort with the federal soldiers, like those judged to have followed *Nde Igaba* out of hunger or gluttony. Part of the reason some natives had begun to also identify the soldiers as "*Nde Ogo, our in-laws.*"

Most people wouldn't consider the circumstance of Lizzy's so-called marriage; all that mattered to them was that "*osorula Nde Igaba, Nde Ogo,* she has followed the federal soldiers."

"They eat better now but the daughter is with *Nde Ogo doing iyakamba...*" some taunted.

Her "marriage" with the soldier might have elevated the status of Lizzy's parents, improving it almost instantly. Egbuta family soon looked favoured in the midst of hungry and starving people desperate for a lifeline.

"Can't you see, nobody struggles with them for anything any longer; won't quarrel with them..." one of my uncles said at a discussion about the family.

"Do you know what the soldier husband can do?"

Some had begun to count the number of times the Sergeant sent to Egbuta family those essential goods which included clothes and even "Nigerian money."

But the Egbutas demurred at the special attention. Some visited the family at night to share from the "bounties." At other times, they didn't hesitate to join others in the daytime to argue how "Lizzy should've struggled with the soldiers a little more or run away," when they accosted her.

Chapter Eleven

First, it was intermittent loud sound of the shelling. In a few minutes the frequency increased and then in torrents. Either the bombs or the shelling guns whistled a tingling sound, flew overhead, in the sky followed by earth shaking landings in seemingly close quarters. Everyone was running, including those who already had put off their clothes and were inside the stream. They ran out naked from the stream to dodge those bombs and shots flying ceaselessly across Amagbala and the larger Eziufu community that morning.

As they scampered, the banks of the stream were littered with folds of heavily faded clothes, shrunk trunks and other wrappers brought to be washed by the escapees.

Emeuwa had come with his mother and was at the male section. According to him, by the crowd you would think that everybody in Amagbala kindred of about 100 people was at the stream. Females were in their section, the males at the other separated by an improvised blind.

Quite a few had the heart to wear half their clothes on wet bodies before escaping into the nearby bush.

Some hid awhile in the hidden sides of the banks and rushed home to pick up some things before returning to the hideout.

"It wasn't much a trouble for the young ones, but for the adolescent and older, it was more than a mad movie," Emeuwa said.

They had trooped to *Okpokwuru* stream early in the morning as usual for the routine communal bath and washing of clothes. Though they came from nearby kindred settlements, Amagbala kindred compound contributed more being the nearest to the stream.

For being quartered so close to the stream, indigenes considered them as the owners of the stream or rather custodians of the waters and the banks. The kindred compound wasn't farther than 100 metres away from the stream.

"Still can't remember how my mother rushed back home to fetch some things with which we made the escape…"

Before night that day, Mama Emeuwa and children had run further down various parts of the bush, ended up in one wild palm wine tree plantation.

The sun was fast setting. They were inside the bush and wouldn't entertain any thoughts of going back home.

"From the plantation, I could hear sound of the earth-shaking landing a bit distant."

Mother and children appeared stuck in the plantation. Moving from one section of the swampy plantation required some tact to halve your weight while lifting one leg. One step at a time; you take a step and struggle to lift it to another portion. Any forceful attempt led to sinking or getting stuck in one place.

"No matter how light in weight, you will struggle not to sink in the swamp," Emeuwa said.

"Mama and I crawled more of the time."

Night had caught up with them in the struggle. It began to rain, poured from the heavens. Water gushed from the earth at the same time.

Mama Emeuwa couldn't find shelter for the three children and had to pour away some of her items in one big bowl and used it to cover them. She stayed out in the rain until she found a semblance of shelter.

"Would sleep and wake because the flood was welling up to my mouth on top of the log my mother put us."

"Mama, atop another big log near a leafless shrub; guess she was crying or something."

In the morning as they tried to stretch and dry up their wet bodies and clothes, soldier ants from God-knows-where, besieged them with so much determination. It was either the family was on their way, or they had something the ants were looking for. They took chunks out of their weak, wet bodies, and crawled into not-so-visible parts under soaked clothes for those killer bites. They must have been oblivious of the precarious situation of the refugees.

Mama Emeuwa was able to fetch a bunch of dried leaves from dying shrubs and got a flame from neighbour refugees to create a bonfire that drove away the soldier ants. She had given it back to the ants.

After some hours, Emeuwa's father, Mazi Okocha emerged and evacuated them to another end of the bush, not as swampy as the palm plantation; it was upland with big burly trees that had an umbrella-size kind of leaves.

At the "better place," federal Jet fighter planes flew as low as touching the trees. Whether that was a route of the war planes nobody knew.

That part of the bush was on the boundaries of the ancestral land between Amaeke Item and Abiriba, the town they called the small London.

"Each flight came with sound shaking life out of us, caused the earth to quake ceaselessly even after the passage." It could have passed for a 4-9 magnitude earthquake.

"At one passage of the war planes, thought it had happened or we were the targets they were looking for." Everybody shivered like leaves.

"Isn't this death we are running from," Okom Ottah, one of my uncles summoned courage to ask.

In a few days, Papa Emeuwa moved his family yet to another part of the bush where he built a makeshift house.

One morning, sister Oyi was cleaning, and found a snake sleeping beside four-year-old Okonta, the son of Okocha's relative. The viper had spent at least three nights or more with them, it appeared. It was kind of it not to have attacked anybody.

Emeuwa's father poised for a battle fetched his machete and club to defend his family, but the snake crawled away without further push or harassment from the refugees.

Okocha, family and other relatives lived there till the end of the month of October 1969.

Reprieve, they thought had come when Papa Emeuwa received a confirmation message that the family could return to their kindred homestead. In few days, they were back to their house abandoned for about two months. Just like other members of the community did.

Giant spiders had encircled the bungalow with thick cobwebs entangling everybody who tried to find a way in there so much that movement inside the four-bedroom house was slow and calculated. Some rodents had returned. Leakages from the tired, rusted corrugated iron roof made the whole place dingy, humid. Every corner was festooned with all kinds of dust and dirt.

"Thought we had returned to our ways of operating from a permanent home," Emeuwa said. But it came to a head on January 10, 1970.

In the early afternoon of the day, Papa Emeuwa got an alert that a detachment of federal troops had arrived in Amaeke Item community. Next was that the soldiers had come to war, burning houses and arresting people of all categories. Nobody waited. Back to the bush, they went.

The arson would continue for hours under the close supervision of their commanders.

Nobody seemed to know the reasons except the gossip that one of the federal soldiers had threatened, "we'll deal with Amaeke Item people; they work with BOFF people."

Nearly every house in the village was razed while some were bombed to ground zero. One of those was OGB Maduka's modest bungalow tastefully finished and sited at a conspicuous point near the community's central business district.

It was said to have been levelled to the foundation by a bazooka grenade launched by one federal soldier who had since targeted Maduka, one of the foremost leaders of Amaeke Item community.

The house and all the valuables were still burning for two days when people came back from their hiding in the bush.

When Okocha and family made to the bush, they left behind Emeuwa's grandmother, Ulo Elu Onyeaku, who could now be above 82 years old. She had become bed ridden. They hadn't contemplated that she should be evacuated in her paralysed state or that their home wouldn't be intact after all. Lying inside her hut, she didn't know when the soldiers invaded her Amagbala compound; only was alarmed by screamings and blazing flames.

The bed-fast Grand Mama helped herself when death by fire knocked on her door. Grand mama crawled out of her well-steeped mud house, unaided, bruised her badly shrunk skin in many parts including her bald head.

She found refuge in a vegetable garden in the centre of the kindred compound planted by one of Emeuwa's cousins, Dr Eke Onuoha; it was from there she watched her thatched-roofed house and the family house razed to ground zero and others in the compound.

"Under the cover of those fluted pumpkins, tomatoes and shrubs I watched *Ami soja, soldiers, jam, jam, kpuo, kpuo,* finished everything…" the old woman narrated in a fit of trauma

Meanwhile, during the fire, Mazi Okocha and his nephew, Ochu Eke had come from the bush hoping to rescue GrandMa Ulo Elu but couldn't proceed beyond the path leading from *Okpokwuru* stream to their kindred compound. At the time, shots from the soldiers were still flying in various directions some of which whooped pass them as they tried to enter the kindred compound. Even the daring Ochu, one of the adult grand children of Ulo Elu had to run back too.

"We fell many times many times, the number, can't tell as we sauntered towards *Okpokwuru,*" Okocha said.

By the time the operation ended, more than 750 houses had been destroyed. Then, the soldiers herded those arrested to the village meeting centre, *Ologho* Eziufu, for execution. Quite a few might have escaped as they marched them to "Golgotha" kind of place.

Survivors told that "as they shoot and kill one, another was commanded to go move away the corpse; in the process that one is shot too."

It continued until they killed more than 33 people all civilians – male and female of various ages. Excluded from this number were those who perished in the fire. A few others who escaped from the firing range believed some were killed before the public execution. Some of the corpses couldn't be found. Five days after the war ended.

.

Chapter Twelve

Unlike Lizzy and others who were abducted, some ladies sucked up to the federal soldiers. One of them, nicknamed *Baby,* like others of her ilk, didn't live with the soldiers. She had much time with them at the Command Headquarters but didn't become the wife of one. One of her kindred relatives thought that "she was businesslike." *Baby,* from all indications, didn't just "warm her flesh."
Her first time, in February 1969, she went all alone like one trying to reconnect to an old friend. Trust soldiers in war situation; they took the interloper with all suscipion. Some of her relatives said it was like an arrest. But her stay in cell might have helped her or became her launch pad. Only her family knew at the time according to her younger brother, Eme. They had pretended that it wasn't much of a worry unlike distant observers who feared to do anything with the soldiers.
While some natives wondered at her audacity or feared for her safety, others snapped, "*obughu nwami,* isn't she a woman."
Her boldness and strides to trek the whole of about six kilometres or less to go meet the soldier paid off. She had reconciled with them and became accessory for many more deals.
The federal military camp, headquarters of the 1-28 battalion was like a den of lions to many. A sort of where hard and death sentences were delivered. Some had likened it to the slave depot of "no return."
Housed in that big community hospital jointly built by the peoples of Item, Igbere and Alayi towns before the

start of the civil war, the federal soldiers took it over to superintend over many communities of Bende division of Biafra; a degradation that was common with the war. Of course, the once go-to hospital had ceased to exist. Nobody went to Umunnato any longer for medical help. Only to answer to cases or to plead for an arrested relative, they went. Often, for alleged cavorting with Biafrans or their suspected soldiers.

The few exceptions were the cases of young women who provided consort with the hyper-sexual soldiers. They were the type of *Baby* and company. According to her Eme, a playmate of Emeuwa, "she has mastered the soldiers" and often spent days loitering and running her rings at the precincts of the army barracks; sometimes for four days in a stretch.

Baby didn't have a husband or a child to worry about and never had been married. No such restraints or commitments, except perhaps a faint consideration for her family name and whatever was left of her personal reputation. She must have lost her real name Mgbeke to the nickname *Baby*; some indigenes believed that Mgbeke would've had a better reputation.

Uncle Agbai said that her *Baby* nickname was derived from her ways with men a long time ago. He had known her while they all had lived in Aba until the breakout of the Nigerian–Biafran war.

At Aba, Mmom *Baby* seemingly traded on used clothes otherwise known as *okirika* but some suspected that she did this aside "business" of hosting men in turns in her one room apartment. The one she rented from a landlord on Alor Lane of Ama Mmong area of Aba. Though her relatives frowned at that tendency they couldn't do much to dissuade her.

"*Baby* isn't a small girl like that," Okom Agbai pointed out.

Back at Amaeke, she had been accused a "few times of having a go at other ladies' husbands." Of all those, only the matter of Arunma's husband came to the open. Yet it hadn't blown up into a quarrel or scandal.

Mmom *Baby's* mother and Arunma's husband hailed from the same kindred compound. No other matter about her came up for long until the Nigerian federal troops took Item town after which she found her way to them and became a frequent visitor in no time. It was gossipped that the soldiers who first arrested her were "the ones who showed her the way after they played with her."

"One of the days, I met her on *Ugu Kporom* early afternoon on my way to Amaokwe on mother's errand," Emeuwa said.

Ugu Kporom, a rolling hill before Amaokwe, and a median point in the distance between Amaokwe and Amaeke, Item communities was often a lonely parch of the road. Emeuwa and *Baby* went together up to Amaokwe, but she continued.

Baby went again and again that nobody bothered anymore to worry about her whereabout. It was the same period natives feared that people could disappear either by reason of being "taken" by federal soldiers or by the bragging members of BOFF. There was no such consideration or search for Mmom *Baby*. Some of her relatives knew better.

Eme, one of her younger brothers always said, "she isn't lost."

Mmom *Baby* would return with lots — corned beef, salt, milk etc.

It didn't matter to her that members of the community had a disdain for women associating with the federal soldiers. Young women who had started visiting her never bothered too. In no time, her late father's residence had become a kind of rendezvous, a beehive of activities, coarse chatting and long-lasting merriment almost on a daily basis. Morning hours were their most preferred, perhaps.

When they closed a session, some walked away clutching pieces of canned sardine, tomatoes, beef and others. For the starving Biafrans, those were the "essential commodities" most needed to survive.

It didn't take long before those ladies began to accompany Mmom *Baby* for visits to the soldiers. Okom Agbai thought that was actually the purpose of the meetings. "She did her own and pimped for the soldiers."

The number of visiting young women increased without formal advertisement and with little fear of the invasion of *Nde Igaba*. Mmom *Baby* looked every inch and acted like the leader, afterall her home was the meeting point. Together they strutted around the community. Some people "feared" them while others continued to loathe them as people who had gone to do "*Iyakamba*."

They had what the hungry people desperately needed and, access to the assumed "conquerors".

Some days a detachment of soldiers drove Mmom *Baby* and gang back to the community in military trucks.

"Soon some natives started to enlist her help to get a reprieve from the federal soldiers," Emeuwa said.

When they took Egbichi, the new wife of Okereke, it was Mmom *Baby* who facilitated her release. It was said that "she gave them another girl to replace Egbichi." How many times she did that wasn't known but most indigenes believed that she did that often.

Some people had started to think that Mmom *Baby* and the group's rapprochement with the soldiers could reduce or stop the hunting for other young women.

But late evening in March 1969, Mmom Ugo had galloped back into her kindred compound; meandered through the huts and straight into the path to *Iyi Okpokwuru*. She had just escaped capture by some federal soldiers though it was already 5pm.

Mmom Ugo had assumed that the coast was clear when she set out to visit the home of her fiancé. Strolling from her Amagbala kindred compound to Amuda, a distance of less than 200 metres shouldn't have been a worry. It wasn't up to 15 minutes after she came home from her hide-out — the out-stretched community yam barn belt across *Okpokwuru* stream was one of them. There were a number of them around the barn and in the patches of fallow farmland.

"Mmom Ugo comes home in the evening to pass the night, leaves early in the morning back to the hideout," Emeuwa explained.

She had since 1967 been betrothed to one George Onuoha also known as GOC. That year she was still a student at the Eastern Commercial Secondary School, Aba and was billed to pass out the next year, 1968 but for the war.

Her parents and the family of her fiancé had agreed to put a hold on the wedding in the hope that the war might not last long. There weren't any such signs any longer.

Fears of losing Ugo to the federal soldiers had gripped every member of her family after her escape the last time. The contingent plan was made — "hand her over to her betrothed without further delay." It must be done without fanfare so as not to let out any information to suspected informants of the federal soldiers.

"What will be her parent's explanations if the soldiers took her after the in-laws had fulfilled all the marriage rites," a relative of hers had asked.

Two days after, Mmom Ugo was given to her husband who took over the burden of protecting her from *Nde Igaba*.

Select members of the family had assembled in the evening, prayers made by her Grandmother, Ulo Elu Onye Aku, her father and his elder brother, Ottah after which the weddng train moved.

"Bride shadowed under a big umbrella, accompanied by a few people singing soft marriage folklore; they marched from her parents' home to her husband's residence in Amuda kindred compound late evening."

In about 30 minutes, the ceremonies were over; people dispersed in a hurry to their various homes.

Mmom Ugo's type of marriage ceremony was to catalyze a number for the endangered marriageable girls. They quickly happened across other kindred settlements.

Emeuwa's mother always supported the abridged weddings because "no well-brought up girl wanted to be taken by *Nde Igaba*, the federal soldiers and no prideful family wanted the stigma: your daughter is doing *iyakamba* with *Nde Igaba*." She shook her head after that remark and murmured the rest. Some fathers were exclaiming, "I can't stand having my daughter taken by those soldiers, *tufiakwa...*"

Emeuwa's maternal Aunt, Ntachi from Amauzu kindred had also escaped capture by the federal soldiers. She was married off like Mmom Ugo though she was earlier betrothed to a serving Biafran soldier, 2nd Lt. Okoroafor. Now she was off to a new husband, Egburonu, "a bloody civilian."

Later part of 1966, Ntachi was given to Okoroafor who joined the Biafran Army in December 1967. Early 1968 he returned from the war front, Ogidi sector, to complete the traditional rites of his marriage with Ntachi. He hadn't paid all the amount of the bride price when he enlisted in the Biafran Armed Forces. A mini-ceremony was held to hand over the young woman to him and the count down to the evidence of the consummation of the union had started.

"Hope he impregnates her before going back to the war front," his relatives wished.

"If he doesn't come back, there'll be somebody to answer his name," the relatives said.

No further ceremonies, Ntachi had joined the husband who stayed just eight days; a day beyond the permission granted him by his Biafran commanders.

For three months Auntie Ntachi lived in Okoroafor's family house at Nde Alaike, Amaogudu after that the soldier left.

An older Auntie of the soldier always visited Ntachi during the time and inquired if she got messages from Lt. Okoroafor. It was more of a question time. After spending some 10 minutes or more with her, she always asked Ntachi: "how is your body moving you?" The new wife often smiled without a spoken answer but one of the days, Ntachi spoke — "It's me that moves my body."

"Nooo, not like that," she cut in.

"Are you feeling something inside? That's, as if a baby or something is forming?"

"Hmm, not really, not yet...!"

What is happening? All the days he stayed with you? Was my bro not doing it?"

Ntachi's dark face paled until small drops of tears coursed down her narrow bony cheeks. She didn't wait to take the report to her mother. "So these people can't be patient; Okoroafor's signature pregnancy will come *naaa*. Is it by force?" Mama Ntachi hoped. The wait continued' until federal troops got to some parts of Bende division and later, Item town.

Lt. Okoroafor who had since returned to Ogidi war sector was said to have moved to somewhere around Owerri. Nobody was certain, like most stories about the war, some twists, reversals, blanks, tragedies and all sorts reported in the most mercurial ways.

Item town had fallen into the hands of federal troops who were doing everything to take full control. Biafran soldiers though broken would show face here and there and boast about what they would "soon do to the vandals."

Indigenes of Item now dealt with both the federal and Biafran troops.

"Let her return to Amauzu; we need to take care of her, protect her…" Ntachi's family had started to plead.

"The girl isn't pregnant, is she? Who knows if the soldier shall return to us?" They weren't alone.

"It isn't wise to wait; waiting for the Biafran soldier is an uncertainty. Worse, if *Nde Igaba* takes her," the family contemplated.

"Instead of *Nde Igaba*, let her go to this new man. If she gets pregnant, better," Ntachi's people reasoned.

According to Mama Emeuwa, the wedding was done in the night in Amauzu settlement at which Aunty Ntachi was handed over to her new husband. Seven or more months had gone since the first marriage.

The new husband, Egburonu now must not only enjoy the companionship of his new wife but take the responsibility of protecting her from the hunting escapades of the federal soldiers.

"Many like him do all sorts not to lose their wives to *Nde Igaba...*" Mama Emeuwa said.

Auntie Ntachi remained married to Egburonu until the war ended early in 1970. She hadn't become pregnant too. A week after the official end of the war on January 15, some ex-Biafran soldiers had returned to the community.

Those who supposedly fought at sectors like Uzuakoli, Owerri and around Umuahia were about the first. They were nearer to Item town. More batches would come in at various times, at midnight and at about 5.00am. Of those, some had bandaged hands, legs and heads. Some were hard-hearing and behaved like psychiatric patients.

One of those paraded the nooks and crannies of the community, demonstrating fighting positions during his time in the Biafran Army. He wouldn't hear you unless you shouted and went close or devised a sign language.

"A shelling bomb exploded near where he was stationed, tore his eardrum and dislocated his brain a sort of," other returning soldiers explained.

"One often organized the parade around the public squares of the community," Emeuwa said.

"*Lef, ai, lef, ai, ebotua,*" he shouted as his cohorts, some ex-soldiers marched with him.

When they stopped at a point, "stand *at ease, odad arms,*" he commanded. A crowd of boys and girls followed them about — "*Kwa, kwa, kwa,* up Biafra" they clapped and cheered.

"Those of us who hobnobbed with the Biafran Boys Company had fun joining the march," Emeuwa said.

Not all the returnee soldiers participated in the mock parade. Some just smiled away, watched.

As all those happened, one or two of the ex-Biafran soldiers would stroll in telling stories of woes they experienced on the way home even as the war had ended. The returnees were now coming in batches so difficult to count. In another batch of the returnee ex-Biafran soldiers was Auntie Ntachi's first husband, 2nd Lieutenant Okoroafor.

He came in the midnight to his Ama Ogudu kindred compound in ragged Biafran Army pair of trousers, bathroom slippers and a T-shirt said to have been gifted to him at Umuahia by a sympathizer. On arrival at the compound, relatives went shouting, jumping and singing.

Sleep had disappeared from their eyes and those woken by the noise of dancing and singing that broke out. They joined to march round the hilly and stony compound dotted by raffia thatched huts. All they did was to praise God for his safe return and to hail their son for fighting for Biafra.

"Only the brave joined Biafran Army, fought and returned," the relatives mouthed as they moved around with him.

Thereafter they arranged a room to make him settle. One room in his father's rebuilt house was cleared and set up for the survivor.

At about 5am the relatives were still sitting with him in the living room and suggested he should take his bath and get some rest. Everybody had been awake since his arrival. But his eyes shone with brightness like one who took a stimulant.

Intermittently the Lieutenant walked the length and width of the compound like one searching for a lost item. Some relatives wondered but felt satisfied that he returned alive. They followed beside and behind as he walked around. For two days, the former soldier and minders hadn't slept.

He would start a long session of questions and answers like one wanting to know all that happened in his absence. "It's been very long, you know," he kept saying in spite of persuasions to take a deserved rest.

"I trekked from Owerri, hitchhiked two different trucks coming to Umuahia and Uzuakoli to be able to reach home," he said.

"At Akara Isu, Isuikwuato, I hit my chest; after all I'm here near home."

At Akara, after Uzuakoli, he got a vehicle that took him to Okoko, the first village settlement of Item on his way. He trekked down to Amaeke, his home community, another four kilometers or thereabout.

The catching up session, questions and answers had continued for a few days until he began to ask about his wife.

"Ntachi is staying with her parents since you weren't around," one of the cousins answered.

"You people couldn't take care of her for me...? He asked.

"We'll go see her; hope she is okay."

The visit was three times postponed until he went by alone. He was received with fanfare by the in-laws at Amauzu.

"*Hee, Ogo soja, Ekele duru Obasi d'relu*" they rejoiced that he survived after all.

The mother-in-law, Mrs Ojukwu had led the dancing and praises to God for saving the life of the former Biafran soldier. After the celebrations, he was ushered to take his seat at the living room of the Ojukwus. Relatives of Ntachi had assembled; one offered the traditional white chalk, kaolin and kola nuts. The white chalk often filled into a bowl-shaped carved wood bearing a resemblance to a human face symbolized the most traditional and peaceful welcome gesture of the community.

"Visitors are required to run a few fingers through the bowl-shape part and rub at the wrist to show they have come in peace and have reciprocated the peaceful gesture of their host," natives would explain.

A customary practice carried over from the days of inter-village wars. No fighter would kill any visitor or stranger carrying on the wrist the mark of the native chalk, otherwise known as *nzu*.

"Ogom kwanu…?" Biafran Lt. Okoroafor asked with some pleasantries.

"*Aaah, Onobaa…Onwua la,* he didn't survive" the younger brother of the deceased responded.

"*Chai, chai,* sighs; man dies but once, appointed unto man to die, someday, somehow, *Ezi ogo.*"

His father in-law, Mazi Ojukwu died about a month ago; he was one of those killed by federal soldiers on January 10 reprisal attack on Amaeke.

His house was also burnt down like many others in the community. Where they sat was a makeshift done after the destruction.

"May I go to the grave to pay my respect," Lt. Okoroafor asked.

"These vandals, your evil, *oya duru 'nu r'nma, it shall not be well with you…*"

"*Ezi ogo, la r'udo, fare thee well,*" he prayed at the graveside.

Lt. Okoroafor was back so fast to the living room reminiscent of a soldier, to commiserate with the mother-in-law, Mrs Ojukwu. He mouthed his sympathies repeatedly and would rub the back sides of Mrs Ojukwu.

The younger brother of the deceased was making some explanations when Lt. Okoroafor went to sit down.

"Your wife Ntachi is putting up with another relative in Apanu; she isn't yet back."

"Really, isn't she aware I'm back?" I need to see her, need to…"

Meanwhile, Ntachi's family had commenced negotiations with her second husband, Egburonu a week ago after they got a hint about the return of Lt. Okoroafor.

"*Nkwa adagharia la, the tune of the music has changed; we need to also change our dance steps, in fact fast.*" They told Egburonu and some of his family members.

"He came back; not his fault, not yours. Let's find a peaceful way…" Ojukwu's younger brother led the discussion few days after they learnt of the return of Okoroafor. Nothing was agreed on the first day, so the settlement meeting continued very early in the morning the following day after Okoroafor left their home.

Tricky and knotty issues were best discussed first thing in the morning, most indigenes believed and preached.

At the home of Ntachi's second husband, Egburonu, Ojukwu Jr had begun, "Ogo, we've to settle this matter before any other thing happens…"

"We can't collect bride price twice on the head of one maiden. The bride price, *isi ego ya,* we'll return and others; please take everything as it has turned out," he pleaded.

"It's nobody's fault. We acted for the good of the young woman. We've to save her again and, our face."

Egburonu had quickly assembled some elders of his family for the meeting.

"As it is, *uka a di igbidi r' onu, it's a heavy matter, not light,* nevertheless, it can be discussed; there's no matter that can't be negotiated, no matter how knotty," one of the elders had enthused.

"We may not have done things so well; didn't we think like human beings? Please, accept our plea. To marry her to you was induced by the war conditions; it's over now," Ojukwu Jr. further pleaded.

Elder brother of Ntachi's second husband, *"ayi anula,* let's review things a little bit; let's discuss again on Eke Ukwu."

"Aaah Ogo, let's not drag this matter; that's eight days from today..." Ojukwu Jr answered.

"Let it be at Eke nta... four days from now," he responded.

At night of that day, Ntachi sneaked to see her mother at Amauzu, pleaded to be left to marry Egburonu, her second husband.

"Chineke ekwetukwa, eluu, abomination," Mama Ojukwu retorted. "That will be evil, you know; fidelity in marriage is in everyting not only sexual...."

"Ogo Okoroafor didn't die; he's with us *nwam.* We've to do the needful; *maka echi, because of tomorrow,"* Mrs. Ojukwu said.

Ojukwu family visited Ntachi and Egburonu two days after; couldn't wait for the fourth day. As usual, it was about 5.30am. They were the ones who woke Ntachi and the husband.

"Ntachi, we've to tell ourselves the truth; we've made a mistake and we've small time to correct it, no matter how painful. Egburonu, if it were you ...?" Ojukwu Jr said.

Every place had become quiet, and Egburonu and Ntachi bowed their heads. This heart-to-heart discussion preceded the one other members of Egburonu's larger family participated in.

Soon, others streamed into their apartment, and joined the discussions.

Voices rose, some stood up but one of the elders said "let there be peace, let there be peace, let's settle" others murmured their responses.

"Ntachi will leave; she will," the eldest of the Egburonu's family said. They excused themselves along with Egburonu for a tete-a-tete and returned.

"We want to find a solution. This won't cause a fight between our two families. Won't it be nice to keep our relationship no matter how it started?"

"Ntachi's younger sister, Egbichi is of marriageable age, isn't it? My younger brother would like to take her in place of Ntachi; we want to remain as *Ogo*," the eldest said.

"Haa, *obu elegh anemeya, is that how it's done?* Ojukwu Jr asked. "Is it what Egbichi wants; are we going to force her? We need to ask her, need to ask her…"

Two days after, Egburonu family led Ntachi back to her parents' home at about 7.30pm. But they won't collect the refund of the bride price, which was one Pound, and ten shillings.

The following day, at about 6am, Ntachi and the family were at Amaogudu with Lt. Okoroafor.

The former Biafran soldier had woken to receive them, showed them to seats in the living room. Ntachi quickly knelt before him, held his right hand.

Okoroafor waited, gradually withdrawing his hand until he was done and returned to his bedroom. Members of Ojukwu family didn't see that as a good omen. The younger ones started to move up and down the room and eventually into the kindred compound, discussing. They consulted Okoroafor's relatives and the elderly among them.

"What do we do? Please, we want an amicable settlement…" Ojukwu Jr said.

"Let's discuss, no matter how bad a matter is, dialogue is helpful," he continued.

One of Okoroafor's uncles had come over and knocked on the door of the room Lt. Okoroafor was in after calling him for a while without getting a response.

The elder knocked again, opened the door, moved in. They spoke for upwards of 20 minutes before Okoroafor followed him out.

The Ojukwus continued their plea, explained the circumstance of marrying Ntachi out in his absence.

"Very sorry, we acted like human beings; nobody knew tomorrow."

Ntachi was again on her knees, crying and pleading along with her people. Mrs Ojukwu had joined and on her knees.

Lt. Okoroafor hadn't spoken all this while, but his relatives had begun to share the palm wine, roasted meat and kola nuts Ntachi's family had brought.

The discussions, pleas appeared better done with some drinking and eating. It gave Ojukwu family some reprieve that their hosts feasted on the traditional small chops they brought.

When they got set to leave, the Ojukwus were pleased that Okoroafor didn't ask Ntachi to go with them.

Chapter Thirteen

Papa Emeuwa came home shivering. All the bravado to hide his broken heart was betrayed by the tiny drips of tears coursing down his sunken cheeks. You had to look closely to take notice. He had returned from the meeting of the war council, the 29 Committee some minutes ago.

As a member of the Council, he participated in the overnight meeting that ended in the early hours of that day of February 1969. The one at which a decision of life and death was said to have been taken.

The council had to decide a response to the ultimatum of the federal troops regarding the "hand over" of one of the community's most prominent sons, Mascot. He was on the wanted list of the federal soldiers.

Okocha, respected and often addressed as Amadu because of his claim to renowned ancestry and forthrightness, was required to brief some elders of the kindred.

He arrived *Ime Ezi*, kindred compound and in his home, but was unable to look those *Nd' Ichie,* in the face. His eyes were already swollen and reddish. But he kept rubbing them perhaps to disguise the trouble he had in his soul. The eyes of a man, like the mouth, would always reveal the travails of his heart. Papa Emeuwa stood awhile and sank into his old mahogany wooden chair in his living room furnished with those decaying cushion mattresses.

Amadu looked up, wiped his eyes again, and squared up to show himself as *dimkpa,* a courageous man, to begin the formal briefing. The elders were waiting.

Leaders of the community took the decision hopefully, to forestall a village-wide reprisal on Amaeke.

Only the "handover of Mascot to a military court for trial could stop it," Amadu informed. The community's initial plea had failed woefully to the consternation of the people.

According to the federal soldiers, "Mascot and a few others had been implicated for helping BOFF fighters" suspected to have intermittently attacked the federal soldiers. And now poised to revenge, the military command demanded to have him. Failure to do so would invite "vehement reprisals that might lead to the destruction of Amaeke Item village and people," the Command maintained.

Either way, it was an uncanny decision to make in the first quarter of 1969 or thereabout, as the war intensified and Biafran soldiers faltered in defending Amaeke people.

It wasn't in the consideration of the people that the soldiers demand would require physical presence of Mascot who was considered a great community benefactor.

"How it came to this; to send him to that den of lions, I can't imagine!" Papa Emeuwa said to himself and watched to see if any other person was listening.

"Well, don't think there's a choice; if we don't, we all die... if he goes, perhaps he dies for us, they spare us!"

If the *Nd'ichie* had been following, it wasn't clear. Meanwhile, Emeuwa who had brought water for them hid in the adjoining room to the living room where they all sat. He was stretching his neck and shaping one of his ears to hear well.

"My stomach rumbled as I considered the gist; though I always liked to listen in but this one...," Emeuwa said later.

A number of times in the past, they had ordered him out but this time they appeared so engrossed to take notice of his shuffling.

"I moved occasionally to ease my awkward standing," Emeuwa indicated.

"Began to imagine all sorts; what's it they are even talking about?"

Understandably, the war council members had taken the decision with deep pain and dilemma. It could pass as the most unravelling of its decisions.

"Isn't history about to repeat itself on Amaeke...?" Amadu further asked rhetorically. Since he started, he hadn't been very audible.

Meanwhile the elders had begun to recall how the British colonial government carried out a reprisal against Amaeke Item community in 1914.

Some indigenes were alleged to have scuffled with *"Nwa Bekee"* white men, members of the colonialist government, over-powered and buried them in a lake known as *Odoro Gburu Gburu*. The only such lake in Amaeke Item, and located in the valley of Amauzu, one of the hilly clans of the community.

Fifty-five years after, Amaeke and its people were again sliding to another confrontation with authorities. This time, it wasn't clear what Amaeke people did, and the confrontation, not also with colonial Police but Nigerian military authority. In this tangle, the British weren't in the front but covertly; with their tacit support for the government in Lagos and its troops plundering the whole of Eastern Nigeria, renamed Biafra.

Part of the allegations against Mascot was that he was bankrolling the operations of Biafran Organization Of Freedom Fighters, BOFF, against Nigerian soldiers.

Often, it was spoken how *Nde* BOFF carried out guerrilla attacks on the federal troops at various locations. For real or part of the war propaganda, not many could confirm.

It was feared that if Mascot wasn't handed over for trial, the soldiers would do worse than *colonial nwa bekee*. So, as the military command maintained their position on the ultimatum, it effectively raised to the boiling point the heat of the civil war on the community.

"Anyway, we've seen the young man off; hope it wouldn't lead to his death?" Papa said audibly.

"You said...?" one of those elders in audience asked.

"Mascot is on his way..."

Everybody kept silent.

Whether he would become the ransom to spare the village of the wrath of the federal military might, nobody was sure.

"Is he going alone?" Another asked.

"Two of us escorted him to *Ugu Kporom*..." leading to Amaokwe from Amaeke, towards the camp," Amadu said.

"Would they have mercy and spare him?

"That's what I'm saying... who knows?" Papa Emeuwa retorted.

Most of the *nd'ichie* began to shift from one side of the chair to the other, chewing persistently the *Oji Igbo* presented earlier by Papa's eldest wife.

They sighed in unison and began to talk a bit incoherently and do comparisons. "This war, this war..." they chorused.

A while ago they had prayed, broken the nuts, began to discuss past wars. Nigeria-Biafra war was far different from the inter-village wars or even "*Agha Burma*" the Second World War, they said.

There was nothing visibly left of the defence of the Biafran Armed forces in the area. Neither was there any more formal connection between the community and other Biafrans.

It wouldn't be the lot of the "bloody, vulnerable civilians" to do any challenge. Though Amaeke Item community had a history of producing warriors who had stood up to fight for the nine villages that constitute Item yet this time it was at the mercy of the federal troops.

The only option was to accept the ultimatum of the federal military commanders. The 29-Committee just did that.

In tow, they had succeeded in persuading Mascot to "accept to act as the saviour of the Community, to even die for it."

The leaders had pledged to do "whatever to negotiate with, beg or pay any ransom the Commanders might accept."

Surprising, Mascot was also at the meeting but what would his views, defence or objections do against a majority who were bent on damage control.

He would have to walk about five kilometers or more by himself to meet up with the Federal Soldiers.

"Assuming he makes a detour, doesn't get to Umunnato? One of the elders asked.

"Nooo, he won't; not that kind of person; he's with us, loves Amaeke so much," Amadu answered.

"If it were me, would I accept to…" another elder asked.

Everybody kept mute again.

"It's hard, really difficult. None can predict what may happen… this terrible war" Amadu said and began to cry. They began to discuss Mascot's multi-faceted philanthropy by which he warmed himself to the hearts of the indigenes. "Everybody knows what he can do..." one of the elders stated.

Himself and one of his in-laws, Maduka had led the way in the village-wide philanthropy and communal development, but he was singled out much soon.

Installation and operation of streetlights in all the key public places in Amaeke early in the 1960s were the most visible. The lighting was powered by heavy duty electricity generating machine in his home. His people often spoke about how in the larger part of Bende, they were the only ones that had electricity.

Mascot became wealthy as a businessman operating in Port-Harcourt before the civil war forced him like others back to the village. Many indigenes believed his philanthropy and success in business might have attracted the jealousy of a high order.

Quite early, he built a decent, attractive house in his kindred compound that stood as a landmark. The architecture mimicked the undulating topography that made some parts look as if they were under the surface, inside the ground. The reason most villagers gleefully called it the first *"under-ground"* home in the village.

That was where Mr S. Anya, a squealer, alleged the accused hid *Ogbunigwe* bombs for BOFF members and used his resources to cater for them.

For him now to go meet his accusers, federal soldiers at their den were unthinkable, some had argued! "Something like accepting to be a scapegoat..." Amadu restated.

"Pray history will be kind to us over this matter..."

"Could I've accepted to...? *Obasi d'relu mere'yi ebere.* May the God in heaven show us mercy?"

Mascot eventually arrived at the military camp at Umunnato located at an intersection of Item, Igbere and

Alayi towns at 3.30pm. Neither arrested nor forced. The soldiers quickly took him in as a guest or one they were sure would come. All those niceties ended when he was taken to the office of the Provost of the Command.

Before Mascot's departure, the community had raised a mediatory team made up in part, of people who could speak Hausa and Yoruba or might have had connections with the Commanders in any way possible when they were part of Nigerian federation.

While he was detained by the soldiers, the mediatory team visited several times to plead for his release or amelioration of any punishment they might decide. At one of the visits, the officer in charge ordered, "you must bring his two accomplices and Anya." The Mediators looked on; their mouths agape but didn't give an immediate reply.

However, the soldiers couldn't wait; a detachment of well-armed soldiers came to the village the following day to take those away to their camp including Anya, the informant.

"Why would they take Anya too?" Some indigenes in the know queried. Most had thought he was their friend.

The community had to step up its mediation especially when they took the additional suspects.They got help from highly connected people from other villages of Item especially those who could reach other officers, not in the battalion.

In between, there were speculations of what the soldiers could do to the suspects. Hopes had been raised that they would release them until the negotiators were told "Anya's case is different."

Then the rumour of his early execution began to make rounds in the community, especially in drinking pubs.

Strengthened by alleged confirmation obtained from a drinking pal of one of the soldiers that, "he's gone; anybody who could do his brother can kill anybody."

Things weren't at ease any longer with the people of Amaeke upon receipt of that information.

In a few days a detachment of the federal soldiers from Umunnato Military Command swooped on the community to arrest more members of the 29-Committee.

Three of them were taken away that day. However, Papa Emeuwa was one of those who escaped by the whiskers. He and other members of the Committee would live in the bush for weeks until they could ascertain the operation wouldn't be repeated so soon. The hunt forced the Committee under-ground for a long time. The War Council had 29 members and was the rallying point of the leadership of the community during the civil war.

Every clan was represented in it. In addition, it had the successful, not-so-successful men, leaders of thought and nominees of the Amaeke Item Development Union, AIDU who helped to run the affairs of the community with the Eze Ogo, Eze Onyeike.

They had started to hold meetings in one of the bushes and at night. Members went wearing ragged clothes. At once, they decided to slow down visits to the Army camp. Unlike the days the lead of the negotiators, Ete Onuoha was going there every two days.

"We can resume after. Let's listen to sources," Eze Ogo was said to have advised.

However, they resumed a few weeks after with the encouragement of the *Seriki*.

"Let's not stop, small time is big time with soldiers," *Seriki* advised. He was believed to read fairly well the psychology of the soldiers.

Community emissaries continued to trudge to and from the Army Command operational base at least once in a week until the military authorities stopped the negotiators from seeing Mascot in his cell.

The lead negotiator, the well-placed man, Ete Onuoha Eke had gone to see the soldiers in one of those weeks and on his way back to Amaeke was alerted by calls from the fainting voice of a mortally wounded Mascot on the sides of a bush path.

"Ete Onuoha, Ete Onuoha," the voice kept calling, going faint more and more.

Nobody would've called Onuoha Eke that way if he didn't know him closely. Though much older, Mascot knew him closely as one of the foremost elders who cared about the community and was also a member of the 29 Committee.

"I listened closely, drew nearer and what my eyes saw was totally gruesome, frightening," Ete Onuoha reportedly said.

"Item eeeeeeeeeh..." he shouted, "Item Okpi eeeeeeh" the second time.

Mascot lay in the pool of his blood right there in the bush, the sun had appeared in the skies, heralding the morning of tropical Eastern Nigeria.

The lead negotiator made to run away when he didn't get sympathisers to answer to his clarion call, but Mascot kept beckoning, *"Nnayi Onu, Nnayi Onu...* it's me, don't run away, please."

He was making suggestions for his evacuation, but his voice was getting fainter by the seconds.

"This thing happened last night; I'm just getting some strength," Mascot said.

"Please go to my uncles, my maternal ancestral home, close here..." his suggestions for his evacuation but Ete Onuoha had started to shout again.

"Please don't shout, don't," he was said to have pleaded with Ete as he kept calling for help. The evacuation must be discreet.

The rescue wasn't total. The location he was recovered from was close to the military command headquarters. Ete Onu said that Mascot's relatives from Okoko Item helped to take the wounded to a secluded place from where the help of Nurse, Chief Mba Okpa was sought.

Ete Onu had begun to narrate the situation he found Mascot in. "The knife cut on Mascot's neck was like that of a slaughtered cockerel; the only difference was that it was at the back of his neck."

The knife execution bid by the federal soldiers had given Mascot a slim chance of survival. Nobody was sure that it would bode well with him given the depth of the cut on his neck and loss of blood. Supposedly done in the night in one of the patches of the bush near the Military camp, the informed said. The soldiers had made good their threat to get back at the alleged sponsor of the BOFF.

Many natives believed that if he was "cut at his oesophagus, in front" he wouldn't have survived.

"How they did that without noticing can only be attributed to divine intervention for the lucky man," most villagers believed. All others executed with Mascot died but he had breath to get some help. It appeared the soldiers continued the negotiations as a smokescreen while they had executed him and company.

In preparation for the execution, it was alleged that the soldiers had said "we won't waste our bullets; kill them with the bayonet." They did.

Fear didn't allow the natives to go search for the bodies of the other victims in the bush.

A few eyewitnesses said Mascot must have been brought in almost dead to Okom Mba Okpa from the slaughter ground. But Mba spent hours resuscitating and stabilizing the wounded before he could be transported further down to seclusion.

It was to the *Ogo Ubi*, Amaekpu Item they took him and where he received the rest of his treatment. Very few, key indigenes knew his whereabout until the end of the war in 1970.

According to Papa Emeuwa, "Okpa continued to treat the victim right there, often trekking more than four kilometres to do so."

Mascot needed to stay in that seclusion, away from the prying eyes of those soldiers who clearly thought that they succeeded in killing him.

Ete Onu who was instrumental in Mascot's evacuation and rescue returned to his Amagbala kindred compound and evacuated his own family to the bush. As they "ran" others in the compound joined and a few other neighbouring settlements. They lived a few days in the bush before they were persuaded to return.

Ete Onu had said, "Nothing could stop the soldiers from coming after us; if they had harmed Mascot, they are determined, meant evil. They'll come for us all."

What happened on January 10, 1970, proved that Ete Onuoha was right about what the federal soldiers would do. They had ulterior motives which became manifest that fated day in January, few days to the official end of the civil war. The offering of Mascot didn't assuage their anger.

The miraculous survivor emerged from the seclusion few days after the civil war to the surprise of so many who had sworn, he was dead. The first notice was when it was gossiped that he didn't die after all. Then, were words that he was organizing a "thanksgiving service" at the Methodist Church, *Nde Okoroha,* the location of the community's business centre.

Many couldn't reconcile themselves with the news and waited anxiously to see how it would unfold, "if indeed he didn't die."

On the agreed Sunday date, the Church was filled to the brim and overflowed such as never happened before. Many sat outside under their umbrella including torn ones. Not even during the annual harvest and bazaar had there been such patient and enthusiastic crowd.

When he emerged in the auditorium with a neck so deep a cut, one he turned with some strain and slowly, the audience erupted in ecstasy.

"Chai, Chineke d' ebube, Obasi d'relu d'egwu, God is glorious and wonderful," many shouted as the Priest tried to calm the atmosphere. It was an impossible thing to do.

In a few moments, worshippers barely sat down, beat drums, tables, chairs, gongs and anything that could produce sound. The Priest resigned to the tumultuous eruption until most people felt satisfied and calmed themselves. All the while Mascot stood on the podium of the auditorium meant to accommodate at least 500 people, beaming smiles of approval, satisfaction and gratitude.

Then he got the audience he required to give his testimony.

"I was dead, really dead but God said no, big no; gave me back my life. Would you imagine that I'm still in the land of the living," he said.

He turned around, backing the audience and facing the altar — the knife-cut wound in full glare, and everybody looked intently at the depth of the scar, dumbfounded.

Some cried and kept busy wiping their faces, others cringed at the sight of the wound.

No speeches, only a song of gratitude and description of the saving power of God. That was all Mascot could do at the time.

"Otudaram'udo ndu, Otu dara mu udo ndu… he sent to me the rope of life, in His mercy" he sang, and everybody joined, singing and crying for joy. Many looked on, folded their arms, shaking their heads and looking at each other, speechless.

After the song, he showed the wound once again to various blocks of the large audience and said, "I thank God" many times and to all those who prayed and supported him during his treatment. He ended his testimony by announcing a change of name.

"Nobody should call me Mascot henceforth; I am Chidi, I'm Chidi, there's God, there's God.

"Sincerely, nobody should doubt that. He's the reason I'm alive and with you in Amaeke."

Chapter Fourteen

Enyidiya could have been the youngest of the many that went missing in Amaeke. Before her case, only adults were said to have disappeared. Many of them were young and middle-aged men. Of the few females, they were traced to the Umunnato Military Command, ever so often. Nobody bothered about those but for the male-folks a search party of relatives combed for their remains in certain parts of the bushes and the ones near the un-tarred main roads. In the matter of Enyidiya, nobody thought that she could have gone to Umuannato to be with soldiers. She was only 11 years old.
For days running into weeks, she hadn't been seen. Some members of her kindred weren't even sure she had gone missing. Most of her playmates in *Umurima Eziufu*, the popular informal association of children of the down part of Amaeke Item, couldn't contemplate her disappearance. Emeuwa, one of the leaders of the playgroup and whose kindred compound was the nearest to hers, had gone a number of times to see her and was told that she went on an errand. The last time, he met one of her older relatives.
"Enyidiya must have gone for her usual business; isn't it what she does? Play a little and run out for all those things that give her money. She must've gone." Emeuwa demurred, and responded, "*Dee*, that's what all of us are doing."
Emeuwa would talk about how Enyidiya often climbed effortlessly, tall *Uha* trees like him, and did early morning runs for African star apples, *udara*, with him. All those they exchanged for Biafran pounds. For these

strides and more, some elderly people took notice and pitied that the children had so early become bread winners. But there was nothing that they could do to ameliorate the situation. One of those had typified *Umurima Eziufu,* as "guerrilla entrepreneurs."

When boys of her age or slightly older waltz through the bush for whatever that could be exchanged for Biafran pounds, Enyidiya was there. Now, many couldn't differentiate her gender and even thought that she was as daring as a lion.

That she had suddenly gone out of "circulation," so to say, could only be discussed by very close relatives and in hush tones. Her blind father, Okom Chukwu couldn't be required to provide any more information, and not even her mother. Somebody had suggested that she "might be feigning ignorant." Nobody wanted to trouble her further because she had *acha ere,* diabetes induced wound; one that had turned Enyidiya into an herbalist of a kind. She was always going to the bush to harvest the prescribed herbs for her mother's treatment.

In the early part of the last year of the civil war, Enyidiya had begun to prime Emeuwa and a few others to join her team to run errands for *Afia Attack* traders. They were so called because of the risk and profitability of their trade across military positions of both the Nigerian and Biafran soldiers. *Afia Attack* traders majored in buying and selling of scarce "essential commodities" such as milk, salt, corned beef, sardine and the related.

At prospecting Emeuwa, she had said, "no fears. We meet soldiers sometimes, yes, and pass them all the time; we just greet them, move on." Emeuwa had started to pay more attention. "Sometimes, they'll look at us ooo, say *kwom* here; knock us on the head, or give us food items and order us back home."

Emeuwa wouldn't join her team. His Mama had told him, "If they kill you, we won't be able to recover your body..." However, Ikoro and Emole joined her. Their brief was to loiter around bush paths near military positions of Nigerian federal troops and Biafrans and provide information. Such information helped the traders to make crossing decisions: decide alternative routes - to wait or retreat. Enyidiya and company got a huge fee for the reconnaissance.

The day they went on the latest mission, Emeuwa didn't know. It was just that "I couldn't see her for long even at Ologho Eziufu, our major playground," he said. Enyidiya and company had gone with the *Afia Attack* traders on a Friday. By 7pm on that day they were already in Okoko Item preparatory to entering the bush through which they would bypass the location of Umunnato Military camp and set towards Ishiagu or Uburu. The reconnaissance team and the traders were making steady progress in the bush until there were gun shots. "Shooting all over..." Okereke, one of the traders said. The crackle hadn't only come unexpected but with some ferocity and for an extended period.

"As the sound of the gunshots whooped through the bush that night huge silence followed; everyone ducked, laid low as usual until somebody screamed." The traders and people who accompanied them retreated further down to hide. *Afia attack* traders, much like smugglers, were always joined by a few others who "ride on their back" to cross from Biafra to territories liberated by Nigerian troops. Such communities might be the ones fully reabsorbed into Nigerian federation so they could live free of war hostilities. There, residents freely bought and sold essential food items. No longer had they anything to do with Biafra and the deprivations prevalent in Biafran territories.

"We're still ducking when the groan of the girl became louder." First, it was — *"Chineke mee..."* then a long shrill cry, *"anwualam mu ee."* Enyidiya had been shot. The lead of the team of three children of the average age of 11 had been wounded. Their fee of about 45,000 Biafran pounds might now go for treating the wound if she survived, even if she was paid more as team leader.

She was said to be in the front of those two children on the upwards side of the path when the bullet hit her right leg. It could've been at about 7.45pm in August of that year, 1969. The traders and their gang believed that the shots were fired by federal soldiers on patrol on a nearby motor road.

Enyidiya had left her Amaeke Item community, some five kilometres away in the evening of that fateful day to continue the "lucrative" service. One, she embraced some months ago. Only her mother was privy to the business and trip though other members of her family enjoyed the returns - the "big" money for the purchase of essential commodities badly needed in Biafra. The Chukwu family of five believed that she was living true to her nickname *"ezinwa"*, exemplary child, given by her mother and fondly so.

The traders and companions were still ducking on one side of the bush. They seem to have run into each other as they made to crawl away from the direction of the shots. "Who isn't here? Okereke had begun. Everybody is panning his eyes right, left and centre. "I can't see Enyidiya, Emole! Can you see Ikoro? Ogbuagu asked. Nobody could say where they had scampered to. "We can't do any search until we know what's happening..."

the traders resolved. All the attention was focused on the one whose life was evidently more threatened.

Enyidiya screams began to ebb just as the traders sighed repeatedly and shivered. Fear of being shot at or arrested by the soldiers was all over them. Every one of them was still darting his or her eyes, and unease. "We've to try, we've to..." one of them spoke up. "This small girl shouldn't die in our hands; she came here for us," Okereke urged.

"It's risky to move; nobody is sure where they are," Ogbuagu said. "Let this girl not die here oo," Okereke restated and set out counting his steps towards the side Enyidiya's screams had come from. *"Hmm, ooh, Lezie kwa anya*, be careful, check oo", Ogbuagu advised.

Okereke took the first steps, his eyes roving to all directions – even leaves caressed by night breeze had caught his attention. He stopped to check; looked up and down branches of the trees. "Smell of human beings must be sniffed," he said to himself as he took further steps in the dark trying to reach the wounded girl who had come on "reccy" mission for them, as Biafran soldiers would term it. In about 150 metres, a receding voice called intermittently, *"Dede, Dede, Dede."* Okereke turned on the third call.

"Dede, it's me," Enyidiya said barely audible that Okereke drew closer to confirm what he heard. She had crawled up to that point. *"Chei...! Chineke mee...,"* Okereke shouted and covered his mouth with both palms. He reached out his shaky hands to touch her body. Enyidiya clothes were soaked in blood. He bent over, lifted the weak body dripping blood and buckled. By instinct, he stopped, sniffed to get some medicinal herbs to help stop the bleeding. Some *"efifia Awolowo"* and others he harvested, squeezed juice out of them mixed with his

saliva and applied them to the bleeding wound. He used some to bandage it with the wrap of strands of cloth.

Enyidiya won't stop moaning her excruciating pain and wished she had listened to her mother's suggestion not to undertake the trip "this time around." Ogbuagu could now join Okereke to lift her body further away. That was after they encouraged Mba, one of their own to stay back to gather and hide the stash of Biafran and Nigerian currencies they had brought for the business trip.

"Where to now...?" They gazed at each other awhile. Ogbuagu said, "lets slow the flow of blood, tie the wound with my shirt and then to Okom Mba in Amaokwe, Item?"

Consensus reached — they would trek about two and half kilometres to the home of Okom Mba Okpa, a notable male nurse whose expertise equalled that of a medical doctor in the estimation of the people. At increased pace, they moved as their remaining strength could support, panting until they arrived at Okom Mba's "hospital" at about 11pm. Tens of people were still crowding to get to the Nurse to attend to them. They did always, day and night. It appeared he was the only medical personnel available, who hadn't joined the Biafran Army or gone into hiding.

"Emergency, emergency, *chetu nu, chetu nu*" Okereke and Ogbuagu chorused and forced an access to Okom Mba. He looked at them and the patient and asked what happened. Before they could complete the story, Mba had started to bring up some bottles of medicaments. How "Dr" Okpa was getting supply of drugs and other medicaments, nobody knew. He managed to stop the bleeding after administering a cocktail of bottled liquids and tablets, stabilized the wounded girl and ordered a bed rest. But there was no bed anywhere and his home wasn't a hospital though many of his patrons tried to make one out of it. You could only beg for a space in the home of some of Okom Mba's relatives and that would preferably be on *okpukpu*, a bed made from clay soil and harden by a fire heating process.

Enyidiya lay there till about 5am until Okereke and Ogbuagu carried her on their shoulders back to her parents in Amaeke, another one and half kilometres via an isolated farm pathway. In an improvised couch, well covered they sneaked her in. Her right leg bandaged and tied to a part of the couch, which was like a folded raffia mat.

Mgborie, Mama Enyidiya raised her hands and screamed. The raffia roof of the house almost lifted with the volume of her cries as they rushed in carrying Enyidiya. She couldn't be held back from exclaiming her fears; the volume of her teary voice still shaking the raffia roof as they lowered Enyidiya in that couch. A few relatives who hadn't gone to farm rushed into their hut. They watched, sat down supporting their jaws with their arms but wouldn't talk.

"Please, please, calm down; don't draw attention to this, nobody knows who is who." The *Afia Attack* traders repeatedly told Mgborie separately. They feared that it might get to the ears of the suspected informants of the Federal soldiers. However, Mgborie kept on but intermittently cupped her two palms to cover her mouth. Now they have to find a way to prevent the information from getting to more people in the community. She was laid in the *nkpuka*, inner room away from the prying eyes of the *ndi-ezi*, kindred people. Mgborie still moaned, grumbled as her tears poured, "…said you shouldn't go, said no, but you refused…" She fell beside the bandaged leg, slapped the floor repeatedly.

When she got a bit sober, "*ekeleduru Obasi d'relu*, that you are even alive; at least I'm seeing you. You've got to stop, yes; you'll get well." She turned to Okereke and partner, "thank you for bringing her back and caring. She's got to stop; know she's trying to help… When she gets well, it's no more. I'm satisfied…" Okereke, drew nearer where she sat on the floor said, "Mama Enyidiya, as it is, this thing must be kept away from the ears of people; for her sake and ours; we're in a war, the enemies aren't far away!" They were going and returned to where Mama Enyidiya sat, "always say she's missing, please."

He and business partner left Enyidiya's house a little after like people who must dodge certain people. They were on their way back to the bush to safeguard their money and to begin a search for Ikoro and Emole who went on the mission with Enyidiya. In Okoko Item, they had begun their surreptitious moves back into the parts of the bush around the community and neighbouring Alayi and Ugwueke. "We've searched the large expanse without a trace to these boys," Okereke and Ogbuagu, the *Affia Attack* traders told an affiliate who lived in Okoko. They had returned to their hideout where they camped in the last three days. They hadn't rested for long before their newsman came with a whiff of developments back in Amaeke - "the boys have been found; they are with the soldiers of the 1-28 Battalion."

"How…? What?" Ogbuagu queried. "They were captured by the soldiers, detained all those days," the informant said. The "newsman" as they preferred to call him said that the soldiers were in Amaeke to arrest "sponsors of the boys; the ones they called informants of Biafran soldiers."

The arrival of the soldiers would get indigenes of Amaeke community either escaping to the bushes or hiding inside their huts. Most had remained indoors and wouldn't risk being shot should they try to run out into the bush. Soon, the soldiers frisked the nooks and crannies of the community looking for the so-called culprit Biafrans who would have sent the children to conduct "reccy" on them. There were no indications they found anything and quizzed the Eze Ogo, village head and the *Seriki*, war time village regent. The *Seriki*, an indigene, always acted as a liaison between the soldiers and the community. Some people believed he spoke Yoruba too as he served as a trading apprentice in Ibadan in the early years of his life. Seriki's mastery of the Hausa language recommended him for the temporary leadership position - One that would grow to compete with the Eze Ogo's, especially in the eyes of the federal troops.

"We shall return," the soldiers told the two leaders and hopped into their two long trucks back to Umunnato military camp. Two weeks after, the soldiers returned as if they were in for a great battle. Many indigenes struggled to connect the "invasion" to any recent incident. A town crier who was up early to do his routine suggested that the soldiers must have been in their positions "before the cockerel could crow." Amaeke Item was besieged! So, it looked.

"They came in four long trucks with soldiers numbering up to 300 or more, and as usual, fully kitted," he indicated. The soldiers ran and jumped to take over the major entry and exit paths of the village. Early risers and those going to farms farther off were also alarmed to meet Nigerian federal soldiers dressed in their battle uniforms, "leaf-like gears" at the exit ways. Meanwhile, a detachment of the soldiers was moving from one *onunkpu, kindred settlement* to the other frisking every house and orchard. They weren't only searching for the alleged sponsors of the "reccy" children but for Enyidiya and Biafran soldiers. Those conversant with the kind of operation believed that the Federal soldiers envisaged a response from the alleged Biafran soldiers hiding in the community. "They followed some tips." Some people claimed to have overheard some of the soldiers say that "a Biafran reccy girl with gunshot wound is hiding in the village." They wouldn't think it was normal, "a sabo might have squealed on the circumstance of Enyidiya," her relatives suspected.

One of the places they quickly went to was Enyidiya's kindred compound, *Nde Okoro*. Every house, room, courtyard and crevice, so to say, was searched with such certainty. The search of the entire village continued for more than five hours; much like a lock-down was being executed on the community. Occasional gunshots but no casualties were immediately known. Thereafter the soldiers drove around to major public squares in the community; arrested some young and elderly men and took them away in their trucks when they left at about 12 noon.

Four days ago, Okereke and Ogbuagu had spearheaded the relocation of Enyidiya. "It's no longer safe for this girl to be around Amaeke," they had said visiting her and the mother. By Wednesday night of the week Enyidiya was gone. The federal soldiers carried out their operation some 12 hours later, at about 5.00 a.m. on Friday. Her relatives had helped to evacuate her and the mother on Wednesday night as arranged by the *Afia* Attack traders. It was said that the traders hired a strong young man who carried her on his back that Wednesday night to Amaekpu Item, an inner village of the Item town, and some two and half kilometres away from Amaeke. Enyidiya's mother and a few relatives followed behind.

Enyidiya arrived at the large compound of an Herbalist in Amaekpu based on the recommendations of relatives. She would get treatment and a cover there; from the prying eyes of federal soldiers and their agents and everybody else. Recommenders had listed the Herbalist as "highly gifted with treating gunshots wounds among others."

Few hours after receipt of the information of the operation of those soldiers in Amaeke, they moved her again. This time, to *Ogo Ubi*, a native farm settlement that was well situated in the middle of a thick forest and hidden away from regular communal settlement. *Ogo Ubi* was reputed to be in a location thoroughly hidden from most residents. Not a few natives believed that it "provided the greatest cover anyone could need." No federal soldier would ever find it, they believed. Some had asked, "how on earth would they reach there? No." An indigene had hinted that it was the same place "they hid and treated Mascot, who was knifed almost to death by federal soldiers early in 1969 or there about. Some of the locals just knew that *Ogo Ubi* was populated by non-natives professional farmers who preferred to be ensconced in the forest, a kind of "settlers of autonomous community" in a settlement.

Enyidiya lived and received treatment there from 1969 until April 1970 adjudged missing, about four months after the Nigerian–Biafran war had ended. Only then could her mother report openly on the progress she made in her recovery and location. They were ready to return home, to Amaeke. She wasn't missing any longer.

"She's better than ever; can walk around without support or crutches." Yet she limped. Her return to and reappearance in Amaeke was heralded by singing, dancing and giving of thanks. Her mother wouldn't let the moment pass without shouting, "thank God with me. *Nde Igaba*, wanted to remove my comfort, *Ma Chineke ekwoo;* had thought she'd lose one leg, but no. *"Nduk'aku*, to be alive is worth more than wealth; still can't believe this terrible war has come to an end. May such be far away from us, never come to us again," Mgborie prayed.

On arrival in Amaeke, some relatives wondered, "thought she was among those said to be missing since last year."

Chapter Fifteen

Many people in the Amagbala kindred hadn't heard until Okom Agbai brought the news of the official end of the Nigerian civil war. As usual, he was the first with the information.
So conversant with news presentations in the BBC, British Broadcasting Corporation and VOA, Voice of America, that he had a whiff of the push to end the hostilities. It had come to reality and as a confirmation of his earlier suggestions.
Agbai had rushed from listening to radio to go break the news to Papa Emeuwa and a kindred uncle, Ete Onu Eke. Both were playing *asigo*, a local table game at a corner of the kindred compound, sitting under the shade of a tree.
Okocha and Ete Onu had taken out the time to rest from perambulating the re-construction sites and a nearby bush from where some relatives helped to fetch wood for the rebuilding of their houses burnt down by federal soldiers five days ago being January 10, 1970.
Okom Agbai's news must've come about 3.30pm, that day, 15th of January 1970; a day that didn't look any different," Emeuwa said.
"*Agha ebuola, the war has ended,* BBC is announcing it," Okom Agbai said laughing and jumping. Those who heard him stopped; even those passing through the kindred compound. Everybody watched his mouth tell the story and demonstrate how BBC relayed the story and the interviews. They seemed not to know how to react but were keen to hear the details. Some had snippets but weren't quite sure of the veracity until Agbai came.

Papa Emeuwa and Ete Onuoha had abandoned the *asigo* game, sprung to their feet with all the light in their eyes, moved forward, backward began dancing, itching to re-confirm.

People were now running in and out of *ime ezi, kindred compound of Amagbala*; some smiles, and breath of relief yet agitated to re-confirm the veracity of the news or re-validation.

"Enhe, so like this; what would happen next?" Some of them asked. Gradually, the immense relief was all over on the shining and grinning faces of the people.

"So like this, like this, all the shooting, gruesome killings of people, destructions, frequent *osondu*, may not happen again. *Ekele duru Chineke,*" they said.

Three cousins were talking, "So we've survived this wickedness; can't thank God enough."

While the information made rounds, those who fetched wood, weaved the raffia palms for roofs or scooped and moulded the clay continued their work.

Everybody was desperate to restore the roof over his or her head, to hasten the return of family members from the bush and the yam barn. They all wanted more cover against the whirling harmattan wind howling across the community.

It was almost five days ago that soldiers of the 1-28 Battalion of the Nigerian federal Army invaded the community: burnt, destroyed hundreds of houses and killed a number of people across age groups. The bereaved had barely completed the burial and mourning of the souls of those so brutally killed in the attack.

In a few days, fresh raffia thatch roofs had dotted the skyline of the community. That much the people could do under the circumstance. Everywhere, pits were dug to produce red mud for raising walls for the houses.

In those pits in every nook and cranny of the community, young men trampled inner soil to bring it to a malleable pulp while others scooped it to the surface. Another set lifted and poured into wall brackets of wood lined in a rectangular form. Soon walls took shape on the marked portions dug around for the foundations of the houses.

As they stopped for rest, "*agha ebuola*" story was all they could discuss. Among the small number were those shouting, jumping up and down and slapping the backs of mates. Others sat, smiling, pondered on how to take the new lease on life. They had lived in the bush since the reprisal attack. Cessation of days of gunshots, shelling and refugee stampedes sounded unreal to the people.

From the reconstruction of residences to the hunt of the news from every angle as the days came. Some ex-Biafran soldiers were returning home from the war and with stories on their way back. Soon, search for ways of rehabilitation, better life and sustenance had begun. Between February and April of the year, 1970, some had migrated from the village.

"*Okom Igwo agala Aba;* Okom Joseph and Thomas are on their way to Enugu; Okom Ogala and Esonu are heading to Port Harcourt, was all I could hear," Emeuwa said.

It was Okom Esonu who said that "some of those travelled with borrowed money."

"Nnem got One pound, Five Shillings from *Nne Nnem Edikaikon* for Igwo to undertake the journey to Port Harcourt." *Nne Nnem Edikaikon* was the nickname of a benefactor of a woman who popularized *edikaikong* soup in the community having had a long sojourn in Calabar before the civil war. Aged about 75, she had huge savings of Nigerian currency she stashed away while the war lasted.

A local safe, made of very thick red clay in her house largely helped to preserve the money from fire. Upon the end of the war, she realized it was a fortune of a kind.

"She loaned money to a number of her Nde Okoro kindred people with which they left Amaeke Item to restart life in the cities," Esonu added to Igwo's words.

Every other thing was restarting including institutions.

Okom Igwo who arrived Aba in the middle of 1970, said that "Churches were early in opening their doors in some badly damaged structures."

Everybody appeared to take to hearty worship perhaps to thank God for survival and to gain fillip to restart.

"It looked logically a right thing to do; right about you are skeletons emitting stench, damaged buildings and gorges dug by bombs," he said.

Some schools had restarted especially the ones sponsored by churches and missionaries. They were followed by public schools, especially the primary.

Not every family was able to send back their wards to school that early. Few that did were those who could find extra money after finding food. Like so many, Emeuwa and siblings couldn't resume that year.

It was one and half years after in 1972 that they registered at the Danfodio Road primary school, Aba where they reconnected with Anyim and Uche.

Anyim hailed from Akanu Item, Uche from Orlu. But they all lived in Ama Mmong part of Aba which held a large population of the city.

Before the war, Emeuwa was at Ulasi Local Authority Primary school, Ulasi road, near the bank of the popular Aba River known as waterside. Now he had been admitted to Danfodio Road Primary School, near Aba stadium.

From class, elementary two he was in 1967, he jumped to Elementary four after disputations with his father. Anyim and Uche were in elementary five. Emeuwa and others couldn't continue with schooling during the war.

In Amaeke Item, some spirited teachers had gathered the children to continue their studies under a large section of a forest reserve known as Ozara, but a jet bomber attack scattered everything.

It was around 11am in 1968, with four classes of children and the volunteer teachers. The earth-shaking sound of the Jet started the melee. By the time the bombs started to explode and the accompanying smoke, nobody knew who was alive and who wasn't. Most people ran, hid, and crawled until they got back home.

A few days after, it was soothing to hear that nobody was killed but that was the end of efforts to school children in the enclave during the war. Most were surprised that the large, tall trees didn't provide enough cover for the pupils and others. Schooling had to wait until the 1970s.

Anyim and Uche had started together at Danfodio Local Authority Primary school from their first year in 1964 and had grown as very close friends.

"For so long, many thought we were biological brothers," Uche revealed.

Their mothers at the then *Ahia Ohuru*, the new market on Ngwa Road shared a shop for merchandising of used clothes, *Okirika* in local parlance. Many would come to believe that the neighbourliness of the mothers had rubbed off on the two pupils.

Emeuwa recalled that like him and his family, the duo of Anyim and Uche and families in 1968 were forced to relocate to ancestral homes when the war intensified. Anyim and the family to Akanu Item while Uche and his to Akokwa in Orlu province. They would from to time reminisce on the devastations of the war especially while they hid in the villages.

"It was common to see unclaimed bodies at road junctions not to talk about intermittent gun battles," Uche said.

"When the war planes attack nobody remembered hunger and anything else..."

"We ran many times to Amaraku, Uzoagba and other places until this thing ended in January 1970. Everybody is back now trying to get up."

At one of the bomb incidents near a market, Mama Uche was killed. Uche had told that it happened in December 1969. A bomb fell on her and other women where they took cover in a gully on the side of the market.

Papa Emeuwa, like many erstwhile landlords in Aba waited for confirmation about the status of his house – "is it standing or destroyed?" They inquired before returning.

On arrival in the hot afternoon of January 1971 on Ngwa Road, a little after Dandikos Cinema, they cast a long shot from Ngwa Road to check.

Father and son jumped for joy and smiled broadly seeing that the bungalow was still standing. On arrival at the spot after about 150 metres walk, they noticed it was partly destroyed.

The damaged part covering three rooms didn't matter so much to them. As they moved around to inspect the property, two occupants of the building who were Aba indigenes stood up to them.

"*Bia ngha, obungiri, ibuu onye?* They asked.

"This is my house! No. 8 Victoria Street, Aba. Why do you ask? Papa Emeuwa responded.

"We are here, been looking after the house. You ran away *na, igbara oso.*"

"You can stay in the meantime, this is my house; the land I bought from Emejiaka family," Papa Emeuwa maintained.

They mellowed and allowed them to continue their inspection.

"We can still be sheltered here, we'll manage…" Papa Emeuwa, Amadu Okocha said to his son.

Bomb attack and exchange of gun fire might have caused the damages to the three rooms and other parts of the 8-rooms bungalow.

"Aren't we lucky? Can't see other buildings; could those bushy plots be numbers 11 or …? Papa Emeuwa queried.

"What would the Landlords do? How'll they restart? This is Victoria Street, isn't it? There are no more buildings on those plots." His misty eyes were still roving.

"We restart at least like this," he had said repeatedly. They looked up again.

"There looks like mini fallow farms. Can you see those ones, heaps of rubbles?

"Let's even thank God," Okocha continued.

In few days, he had settled and gotten further support from his relatives who arrived earlier, later part of 1970.

He took to retail sales of firewood. With one pound, he bought the goods. Papa Emeuwa worked with his son to buy from wholesalers and fetched others from nearby bushes to add.

A good number of returnees must have need of the fuel "to cook…and even to light up homes and warm up at night," he enthused.

"Sales revenue helped with badly needed cash; Emeuwa and I could eat twice some days," Papa Emeuwa said.

For six months or more, it had become fairly good business for Emeuwa and his Papa as more people arrived in town.

That was until competition came. It came fierce with the increase in the number of retailers. It was a competition for survival and rebuilding. Everybody wanted a part of it.

Then Papa Emeuwa began to eye another niche — entertainment.

He invited some younger relatives over to help to construct a make-shift pavilion in the position of the destroyed part of the bungalow. That became the take-off point of his Palm Wine Bar.

"We've got to find other ways; people certainly need a place to relax, think less of the aftermath of the war even if it's temporary," Papa Emeuwa said.

The business proceeds soon matched his forecast and became an instant cash cow. But a number of patrons struggled with drunkenness and those other consequential behaviours.

"It isn't part of my objectives anyway; what do I do...?"

With the increase in income, he quickly bought household needs and began to plan for other members of his family to join him in Aba.

"We should be expanding to the unbuilt portion of this plot; Orji and others in Amaeke to join us here."

Most people believed that recovery from the ravages of the war would be faster in cities like Aba and other erstwhile established towns in Eastern Region. Not to mind that the towns also had broken utilities — no electricity, water, roads damaged by bombs, gully erosion and more. Yet people returned to these cities in numbers.

"They're doing nothing in the village there; everyone should come here and struggle," he had discussed with other relatives out in Aba.

Okocha's third wife, second son and daughter travelled to Aba one month after from Item and quickly integrated in the business. The bar could now provide, in addition, small chops and other needs of the drinking men.

It wasn't a surprise that the bar and his residence had become a rendezvous for so many activities among which was oral messaging, sending and receipt of mails from the village.

As the centre became consolidated for all sorts of activities and conviviality, sales of palm wine, assorted fried meat, and small chops grew much more.

In the evenings, especially, the drinkers would assemble, and exchange "happy survival" greetings as well as make enquiries about old friends and acquaintances.

That way, mutual solidarity and joy of surviving the devastations of the war flowed amid discussion of other issues. More than any other, recovery from losses of the war, and strategies for new sources of income dominated the meetings.

In the process, a number of bottles of the red colour palm wine were emptied into *"who send you,"* big transparent glass cups with a handle, and into the protruding bellies and charged system of the drinkers.

Suppliers, Ibibio and Annang people from Ikot Ekpene were as relentless as the drinkers. They brought them in big blue plastic drums after which the liquor was served in white transparent bottles. Before that *nche,* a colouring substance derived from the bark of a tree had been added. Some claimed it was medicinal, but it changed the colour of the palm wine to red.

Some of the patrons of the bar would often increase their consumption if they earned more money from their day job of off-loading sacks of onions, rice, beans and others supplied by traders from the Northern part of Nigeria.

"One of the few available jobs after the war; hard labour it is but where are the alternatives?" Hyacinth Nwangwa, one of the patrons always said.

Many of them became emergency muscle men using their shoulders and back to off-load those sacks and sought relief and refreshment from palm wine. All the warehouses at *Ahia Ohuru* new market retained them as their off loaders.

Papa Emeuwa was making more money as more drinkers found space to relieve the pains of the war, labours of the day and shared experiences of the 30months Nigeria–Biafra war. The drinkers never failed to review the war even if it was comically.

"Which sectors did you fight in, idle civilian, coward? Go away, you went on AWOL" was a common banter in the bar especially at the height of intoxication.

Many of the patrons were ex-Biafran soldiers who told their stories, sometimes, to claim some superiority or to get extra bottles from the more generous ones.

"*Nye ya* two bottles, *okwara mgbo biko, Agu nwoke*" give him two bottles, a warrior, he fought the Biafran war, one elated drinker would place an order and pay. Then the riotous joy would be heightened and raise consumption of the intoxicant.

Some of those drinkers would stand and fall in line as in a military parade; one would assume the position of parade and war commander:

"*Lef ai, Lef ai, Lef ai,*
ebotua, ebotua;
Position take, fire —
Ka kokoko, ka kokoko… Ka, kom, Igbim"
Everybody would laugh.

"*Overnight*," the name for fermented palm wine, is working; "the power of alcohol," one of the drinkers soberer would jest. Some would hail the people in the parade and increase the applause.

"Bring four more bottles, two on that table, two here…" the sales would continue till about 9pm when they would start dispersing one after another. Some would dose for another 30 minutes, woken by the bar boys to go home, if they had one.

At other times when they hadn't become so tipsy, "this war eeh, not good at all; Ikechukwu didn't survive; his other younger brother is amputated… now everybody is starting afresh."

Sometimes the discussions veered into lost opportunities or interrupted educational pursuits.

"Nobody's talking about going back to school now; let's stabilize first *biko*."

"Well, nobody knows tomorrow." One would sermonize. A number of them were secondary school students before the war started.

Papa Emeuwa looked like the greater beneficiary of the camaraderie — well improved cash flow, income enough to invite over the rest of the members of his large family. They joined him and the business later in 1972.

Some of his children would return to school the same year as Emeuwa when he joined Danfodio Road Primary School. All the while Emeuwa served as one of the bar boys.

Emeuwa was fortunate with the implementation of a new educational calendar that began in September 1973. It used to be January every year. By the change, he did Primary five in 1973 and in September got promoted to Primary six. The following year he gained admission into

Hill Grammar School having passed the common entrance examinations.

Proceeds from the palm wine bar business were all that was needed to finance his education and those of his siblings. The business continued to boom until well after he had completed his university education in 1986.

He, Anyim and Uche had re-united at the University of Nigeria, Nsukka. While Anyim and Uche were in their 3rd year, he was in his first year.

Anyim was in the Jackson School of Journalism while Uche was in the Department of History in the Faculty of Arts and Social Sciences. Emeuwa was admitted to study English and Social studies in the faculty of Education.

It didn't take long for them to rekindle their bond. But a lot had changed. They had grown through secondary school and looked at life differently.

Now and then they discussed how it was with them before the war and the struggles that had followed since the hostilities ended in January 1970. Some of the matters wouldn't just go away. Uche always remembered that the war took his mother.

"We lost her in that bomb attack at Ukwu Ube market when a federal jet fighter bombed the place in 1969," a month before the war ended. But his father survived and was now resident in Onitsha.

"Oh, no…! Yeah, my Mama was devastated by the news and often talked about her bosom friend, business partner. This war …" Anyim responded.

"You must have been luckier," Uche said.

"Not really; the stories are too many and touchy…" Anyim said.

"My Papa had returned to Aba in 1971 but couldn't locate our house anymore. I mean on Agharandu Street," Uche said.

"He arrived on our street, could only "see Numbers 12 and 13, not numbers 10 and 11. Our house was number 11," Uche explained.

Uche and family had lived in their 10-room bungalow from 1962 to 1968 before the federal troops took Aba during the war.

Relatives said that Papa Uche collapsed noticing that his house was destroyed and had to be taken back to Akokwa for further recuperation.

He regained stability in his health shortly after and opted to relocate to Onitsha in 1972 to restart his life. According to Uche, he preferred to be away from Aba, hoping to move his mind from reminders that "he wasn't a Landlord anymore."

Uche stayed with a relative in Aba while other members of the family joined his father there in 1973 to continue their recovery.

One of the relatives had said that Papa Uche in Onitsha joined *ocho passenger* business, commuter passengers' canvassers at one of the numerous parks in the Upper Iweka area. He rebuilt his finances and went back to his original line of business, merchandise of groceries. Relatives said that he made steady progress, remarried and had in 1980 sold the Aba plot of land.

The three musketeers, Anyim, Uche and Emeuwa never failed to reminisce.

"Still marvel at that first bombing, how we survived; didn't know how you ran," Anyim said.

"*Iga asikwa*! Nobody cared when it was *osondu*; every drop of adrenaline pushed to safety first…" Uche clarified.

"Grateful for our survival anyway; imagine those bombings and killings; demise of my mother, greatest regret, I tell you; we can recover other things, not her life and many others."

Anyim caught in, "I understand. Just take heart. We all have to. So many things to endure, many; it's an unforgettable period, really."

"Yes indeed. Endurance, deep scars; how can we ever forget," Uche said.

"But we've to look forward, no matter what. As they say, *nkiruka*... the past is past, the future holds better promise." Emeuwa affirmed.

Chapter Sixteen

Biafran Major Joe returned from the war at the time most people thought he died fighting. It wasn't clear why he came home that late except that it was reported that he could be in the band of Biafran soldiers who didn't like how the war ended or the surrender option.

Some of them, according to those reports had kept fighting in pockets of locations some weeks after the war had ended and only stopped after they ran out of ammunitions.

"Any way, I'm happy he's back with us and alive, that's all," Mama Emeuwa had told some relatives who visited to rejoice with her.

Like Mama Emeuwa, other family members didn't care to know the details of why he came later than others. The four months or more during which they waited looked like ages, but they had been observing the warrior and thanking God. Emeuwa did more. Meanwhile, Mama Emeuwa said that Major Joe joined the Biafran Army in 1967. "He was one of those who did so voluntarily."

Joe could also have responded to the overwhelming sentiment in Eastern Nigeria at that time — resist the invasion of the federal troops and help build the new nation, Biafra.

According to Mama, Joe joined without consulting any family member. Had he consulted "I would've opposed it one hand." Joe was said to have related with Mama Emeuwa much more closely than the rest of the members of the family. The military interventions of 1966 among other reasons wouldn't persuade Joe to pander to the family, some people suggested.

"The two military coups, in January and July didn't solve any problem; they worsened the cohesion and unity of Nigerian federation and created an uncontrollable crisis that culminated in a civil war" the one Uncle Joe had gone to fight on the side of Biafra.

After about a year he joined the Army, 1968, Joe had become a Captain in the Peoples' Army of Biafra at the age of about 20. He enlisted after his course at Yaba Technical College, Lagos in 1966 and a year after his time at Harris Commercial Secondary School, Aba. He got to the rank of a Major before the end of the war.

While most family members had continued to rejoice over his return, Emeuwa had brought up again the matter of his changed physique. He had taken notice of the slight deformity in the gait of his uncle and became nostalgic of the form he thought he saw him in 1968.

"Not sure his body had any semblance of this odd shape," he told some playmates. "Then oo, he stood or walked upright as a six-footer." Emeuwa had gone on an errand for his mother and stopped over at the *Ologho* Eziufu where he met some of his playmates.

Emeuwa was aware that his mother, more than 12 years older than his uncle, had quietly been contemplating the bent physique Major Joe portrayed since he returned.

During the war, in January 1968, he visited to see her sister, Emeuwa and others in Aba accompanied by two orderlies holding one thing or the other for him. He was in his military uniform.

"People in our Victoria Street neighbourhood were alerted by the entrance of a military truck with reinforced tyres that looked like those of a caterpillar; the truck that brought him to the front of our house."

"He looked every inch lovely yet fearsome to behold in the camouflage uniform that resembled the skin of a leopard," Emeuwa recalled.

"Not even the war situation diminished his ruddy body and, fair complexion," the one he shared with Mama Emeuwa and most of his siblings.

His six feet height fitted well into the uniform that rested on his confident broad shoulders, and athletic physique. The jackboot he wore, into which the helms of his trousers were tucked, looked so big and strong you would imagine it could crush stones.

"His appearance created such an attraction to join the army; now he looked not as good as in his last visit." Emeuwa reminisced.

"Sat with him in the living room; as usual hailed Uncle Joe. Quietly, he would retort, "Captain Joe, *inula,* you heard me? Captain Joe Igwe Nkuma, the stone.*"*

His visit was the second and the last time he came to see the sister in Aba.

"He held me to himself as I kept busy running my fingers on his uniform, feeling the texture and touching repeatedly the Biafran sun emblazoned on it."

"The military faze cap he wore sat nicely on his head but covered his luxuriant eyebrow a bit."

Intermittently, Mama Emeuwa came to him; shed some tears as she continued with preparing a meal for him and his entourage. Twice she stopped, stared at him and asked, "Jonah, must you be in this war? *Ibu kwanu nwanta,* you are still a child."

That much time he spent after a hurried meal and said he was going for a "meeting at the School of Hygiene, Aba" which also served as a war office.

Since that departure, Mama Emeuwa didn't get a message or letter from him; except that some Biafran soldiers on AWOL brought snippets about his affairs. They were often about what happened two or three months earlier. "Saw him at Nkpor, Onitsha sector, Owerri sector… he is a big soldier oo… and stories like that," they told.

When the information stopped coming, Emeuwa's mother resorted to prayers for his safety. She invited a few prayer bands to intercede for him and some relatives. She was often in the home of some Priests of the Methodist Church to supplicate for his wellbeing.

At the end of the war in January 1970, Mama Emeuwa, like others hoped that her brother would come home early.

Her expectations and trepidations heightened with the news of the arrival in Amaeke Item, of the first batch of the former Biafran soldiers a few days after January 15. Mama visited the homes of those people, their parents and returnees hoping to get a clue about his whereabout or circumstance. The number of returnees Biafran soldiers increased, and Mama Emeuwa was reminded of her younger brother that hadn't returned.

The month of January had gone; February, March went so fast. The month of April came and was going too. It ran so fast so to say, and Uncle Joe hadn't been sighted. Neither was there any concrete news about him, dead or alive.

Mama Emeuwa began to have moments of tearful solitude. Any former Biafran soldier she saw triggered a session of sobbing. She so cried until the early hours of 28th of April 1970.

A relative had run all the way from Amauzu, the hilliest part of Amaeke, about three quarters of a kilometre away to her Amagbala Eziufu quarters to alert her. It was about 6.45 am.

"Your *soja* brother, Joe is back."

"He got to our *Nde Nkuma* family house at about 4.30am, today, today" the messenger affirmed.

"Are you for real…?" Mama Emeuwa asked and stared at the harbinger of the news?

Soon, she began singing and dancing, and ran the length and breadth of the kindred compound.

There she went with her favourite song, *"Iga s'imu efelaya, obugi g'emerem ihe ona emere mu o?* Why wouldn't I worship God, who can do what He does?"

Mama Emeuwa stopped, ran inside the house to change her clothes to go to Amauzu ignoring the beckoning of Papa Emeuwa who sat out with some elders in the *obu ezi Amagbala* that early morning.

She hadn't climbed the hill leading out of the compound, *onu mkpu*, when she sighted her brother walking towards her.

She ran so fast and flew into the embrace of the returnee Biafran soldier that the two of them almost hit the ground. They locked themselves in that embrace and gravitated back to Amagbala kindred compound.

Many people had rushed out from their homes, assembled at the main bowl to behold the Biafran soldier. It was as they chuckled that it became clear that most people had concluded that he "died fighting."

"This man has come back to life," the jubilant people chorused even in audible voices!

Soon, he joined the elders where they sat having been offered a seat. They shook hands with him vigorously, hugged and told how his grandfather, Nkuma was also a warrior of note.

"It was the first time I heard that; Mama never shared this bit of information," Emeuwa said.

Some called the returnee Biafran soldier, *"ochiagha,"* war commander of note. He acknowledged, raised his right hand slightly unlike politicians would do. He would further respond, "Yeah, major" which was his last rank before the war ended.

Calmly, Uncle Joe, rather Major Joe, spoke to them – counting his words, grinned and nodded as he chose and looked like one cultured to measure everything, his thoughts, remarks and responses.

His time with the elders ended in prayers for his continued safety urged by Emeuwa's father, Amadu Okocha.

Major Jonah stood and saluted the elders as soldiers would and proceded to his elder sister's home to eat the food she had busied herself to prepare.

He ate and licked the plates; he must have been very hungry. He hadn't eaten in days as he would later disclose. The ex-Biafran soldier chatted Mama Emeuwa, the elder sister and stood to go back home.

"Watched as he stood hunched; his steps were fast and far-flung. I followed to see him off; he appeared taller anyway," Emeuwa said.

"I didn't struggle to match his long pace; preferred to follow because I was keen to observe his new gait - bushy hairs and beards, a bit emaciated but looked rugged."

"He kept breezing past people as I ran after him. But I was wondering why he was bent over as he walked; like one looking for something on the ground or those old people in our village?"

"Isn't he Uncle Jonah?" He tried to reason.

He escorted him to the central business district and beat a retreat; not without a promise to visit often. Major Joe beat Emeuwa to it. He was always in their home to eat.

As an orphan and without a wife, he preferred to eat in the home of his sister, the nearest to him. His two other elder sisters lived three or four kilometres away.

Emeuwa had been meaning to learn something about the war from him. And why he now walked bent. As Major Joe sat, spreading his legs and reclining on an old chair after a meal one of the days, Emeuwa asked, "Uncle, what did you learn from the Biafran war?"

He went taciturn, rolled his eyes and faced down awhile. He raised his head slowly and looked straight into Emeuwa's eyes – "war is not good; we had to, but it isn't good at all. Let's hope it has ended. Not good." He had another question.

"Why didn't you come back when others came?"

"When did it really end? When, when... leave this matter!" The ex-Biafran soldier answered.

"It's okay Uncle. Why do you walk the way you now do? Emeuwa further asked.

"How do I walk?"

"Huuuuh..." Emeuwa went quiet and restarted.

"Like somebody looking for something on the ground."

"Hahahah... hurhurhur" Major Joe retorted.

"You won't understand, yes. Those trenches – narrow, shallow, deep and not so deep; manned heavy *ati-mgbo*, hung artillery guns on my shoulders over long distances, long time. We didn't have vehicles; maybe that's the mark", the returnee soldier said.

Major Joe as he liked it, "you did? You mean nobody could help you?" Emeuwa asked.

"I was their leader, had to show example. No problems."

"Now you are hunchbacked; I don't like it."

Uncle Joe turned, focused his bulging eyeballs on Emeuwa for upwards of sixty seconds, deposed," don't worry, I'll be fine; one of those things."

"You feel this way because I'm alive; the dead don't have deformity. Do they? "It's okay."

He stood up, called his sister, "**Mmo** Ebuonye, thanks a lot. I go...."

"As he walked off, my uncle, Major Joe was still looking bent over, hunched at his back," Emeuwa restated.

When he took the walk Emeuwa thought he was angry but two days after, he was back in their house for the usual things.

"This time I wasn't quite disposed to engage him in a discussion, but he started one."

He went back to the questions Emeuwa asked last time around – "don't want us to discuss the war more... what'd you understand at your age; not good..."

"Can't talk about everything... if we do, one may lose his mind," Uncle Joe said.

"If we knew it would end like this, there would've been no need; the cost is much. Well, let it be."

"Let's hope for the better... *nke dirifu ka*, tomorrow holds better promise," Major Joe surmised.

As he stood to walk back to his home, Emeuwa again fixed his eyes at his new posture. He was now, something he wasn't born with or wasn't part of his physique until he had served in the Biafran Army.

Few days after, Papa Emeuwa and elders and others of the Amagbala kindred gathered at the *Obu*, their general meeting hut. They exchanged their usual banters as they made to sit.

The younger ones were busy greeting the elders, *"nnawo"* and they answered *"ibola, unu abotukwa;"* those customary greetings. Done with those, it was time to consider the most important item on the agenda of the family meeting: "account of young people who joined Biafran Army, how many returned and how many haven't?"

Before that, the kola, *Oji Igbo*, specie also known as *abata*, must be broken in the most traditional way.

Nnanna Owoh, the eldest stood, took one nut; he broke it with all the traditional dignity, and it had four pieces. A smile on his face, he placed them on the left palm of his out-stretched hand and on right held a gourd filled with palm wine. There he stood about a metre away from the rest and began to pray.

"Obasi d'relu, Onye kere uwa…God of the heavens and the earth"

Next, he called on the spirits of the ancestors, *"nde ichie Amagbala, Nyari Aegburu…."* Grand Papa Owo then prayed that the meeting will proceed well as they discussed the affairs of the kindred.

He returned to his seat; a long bench made of hardened red mud others shared with him. They hailed him, *"ilua woo, Oke mmadu."*

Now they can begin the census of the men who went to fight for Biafra, going by traditional homesteads of *Ime Ulo and Onuzo ulo, immediate family and aggregated families.*

Each lead of the smaller family units was required to give names and numbers and any other details that might be needed. They did so one after the other.

About one hour was gone, amid banter and ancient stories of inter-village wars, yet they took the census.

"What of Eke Ottah Ottah, *oka alua*, he isn't yet back. Orji *kwanu*, he isn't back too, *Igboko nta kwa nu…*" they went on and on.

Of the nine young men who joined the Biafran army at various times during the war, four hadn't returned.

Of the lot, the matter of Eke Ottah Ottah stood out. He was already an undergraduate of the University of Nigeria, Nsukka where he was studying engineering. His immediate family members denoted him as "the most handsome of the children of his generation."

Eke was a six-footer, very fair, grew dark luxuriant afro hair — he looked every inch promising from all that the eyes could see.

The most prominent missing Biafran soldier of the kindred was in his early 20s like the rest, when he joined the army late 1967. Last information received about him was when he fought at Onitsha sector.

"He is a big soldier oo; doing well; saw him when they were moving us to Owerri in 1968," one former Biafran soldier had told that year. Nothing else about him was heard until the war ended in 1970.

Done with the census, the elders inquired if the families made sacrifices for the yet-to-return Biafran soldiers at the *Afa Amagbala shrine,* the deity most of the people believed could protect members of the kindred.

"Yes, we did, after they had joined the Army," relatives confirmed. Okom Jeremiah, one of the elder siblings of Eke Ottah Ottah answered.

Emeuwa had come to pass a message to his father who sat with those at the *Obu*. He wouldn't leave immediately. *"Yes,* we did the sacrifice, infact Nne Eke did another one in 1969, Jeremiah added. Papa Emeuwa turned to his son and urged him to get back home quickly to deliver his response to Mama Emeuwa.

Chapter Seventeen

A few of her former playmates had sighted her alight from a white-colour commuter bus at the community's business district. They were about 100 metres away and only waved at her. A hand luggage and a lady's bag strapped across her shoulder was all she had. It was as some of the traders at the market were closing and retiring home. In that twilight, Lizzy walked briskly out of the district, took the back pathways to her Agbonta homestead. It would've been a shorter trek for her if she followed the main road. The month of June 1970 was just beginning.
She had been indoors since that day and wouldn't do things with members of her kindred. One week had gone but only a few of her people took notice. It didn't take long for those to speculate about her affairs.
"Was she the one I saw on the way from *Iyi,* stream?" One of the ladies had asked. More questions came up a few times before they could confirm it was Lizzy, the one a soldier abducted and married some months ago. "Maybe she is pregnant; the soldiers didn't come with her this time!" They gossiped. "She must need her mother to nurture her and the baby in her womb; it's okay. They don't hide pregnancy, do they?" The longer she stayed in Amaeke, the more convinced they were that she wasn't pregnant or maybe pregnant of personal troubles.
Her husband, Sergeant Aminu, Emeuwa learnt had been transferred to a Brigade Headquarters in Abeokuta, Western Nigeria. Another relative of hers and a confidant of Seriki, war-time Regent, confirmed that "for about five months, the soldier hadn't communicated with Lizzy

and didn't send "signals to her," as soldiers often say. Then a rumour went on; it was seeping from the banter of barracks people that the "Sergeant will get another wife there." Another had added, *"That one, no be problem."*

One of the days, a soldier at the precincts of the barracks asked Lizzy. *"You still dey? You don get the signal?"* She had waited for such a communication with her husband for this long without success. Her suspicions had grown with the receipt of those streaming gossips. Some she heard first hand. Lizzy had gone to see the leaders of the wives there and returned to her apartment. If the meeting was comforting, it wasn't clear. Moments after, "I will try to get a pass to visit home ..." she was said to have confided in one of the older women. A few days after, she took permission to go to the nearby market near Alayi where she had earlier moved her baggage to a shop. From the market she trekked farther, about three quarters of a kilometre to board a bus coming to Amaeke. The story changed, "a soldier's wife has gone on AWOL."

Emeuwa had been going to Agbonta but hadn't seen her. Another time he went in the evening. Lizzy wouldn't like to hold lengthy discussions; obviously inclined to more discreet meetings. Sanguinary Lizzy had suddenly gone reserved even taciturn. Her parents had started to get worried about her new ways and her so-called marriage that was "on trial."

"Nobody knows how our soldier in-law would take Lizzy's departure" Egbuta, her father was said to have contemplated. He went looking for advice and guidance everywhere. Every piece suggested that he must consult with Eze Ogo and Seriki.

"If the Sergeant doesn't come in the next two months, consider the marriage to be over," Seriki had said in the

Obu of the village head. Eze Ogo smiled, threw his hands up said, "Egbuta, *okwa inula,* be guided." Egbuta stood transfixed and stared at the floor awhile; he shook his head as he left, returned home. The man of the house, however, appeared inclined to finding his own contingent solution not minding what could be the soldier's response. His relatives were offering their own advice privately and seemed to have regained their voices.

"Once this time passes, she may leave Amaeke, go to Aba; *even sef* the war has ended," Egbuta said. There was the view that some of his relatives might have muted their support for his bolder stance. One of them, Egburonu had said, "Dede, I like the way you're taking this matter now. How I wished..."

Egbuta would continue, "by the way, did he do anything on her head...? Those gifts are nothing according to our traditions." Lizzy's mother was on the side muttering, "if the man is no longer interested, will she wait forever, tell me, *eeh?* This's something we entered into because of gun; you can't continue to wait. *Onye obula ya jo isi onwe ya,* everyone must find means of survival."

Before the expiration of the two months, Lizzy was ferreted to Aba as it were, to go live with her Uncle Igboke Egbuta. "My daughter has suffered; this is a 13-year-old ooo...the earlier she puts her mind into other things, the better for her development. She alone can't bear the wages of this war," Mama Lizzy added.

The following day, she walked her daughter to the house of a benevolent indigene travelling to Aba in the next few hours. The escort would hand Lizzy over to the popular driver and transporter, Okom Dani on reaching Aba. Most indigenes believed that Dani would always deliver their messages. At about 3.30pm, the bus she travelled in pulled up at the garage on Ngwa Road, Aba. Lizzy had forgotten the address of Uncle Igboke's house, but an Amaeke man invited by Dani knew her uncle and residence and volunteered to lead her to Obohia road off Ngwa Road, Igboke's residence. They hadn't walked 300 metres of the one-kilometre distance when Lizzy started to talk. *"Dede,* see so many people, moving like maggots; plenty motor vehicles, houses." The guide, Okom Dike, laughed awhile, said, "this is Aba *naa,* Enyimba city." He was still laughing as they made a left turn into Obohia Road. "Amaeke isn't like this, the barracks too; all these motors moving," she said. Lizzy and Okom Dike had arrived at the multi-room bungalow her uncle lived in, said to have 30 people as tenants. That evening, most of them had come home. It became a chatter box. After awhile, the noise smothered, and each tenant tended to his or her room and one trade or the other to make up for livelihood.

For the few days that she stayed home, Lizzy walked up and down from inside the yard to the front to watch passersby: people riding their bicycles, a few motorcycles and those Lorries that transported people from one hinterland to the town. Uncle Igboke would devise that she would be working in his tailoring shop, six buildings away. "War has ended, *onye obula ya agba mbo,"* he advised in a meeting with her and other members of his household. As she went up and down from the residence to the shop, "this Aba is interesting ooh," she said, smiling. A few relatives had started to guess that she was acclimatising fast or recovering from the trauma of co-habiting with the soldier at the tender age. The flutter wasn't hidden. The gradual revival of her outgoing spirit might have helped in her quick integration including friendliness with male and female folks. She could be in the running for a popularity trophy in the first one month if there was a contest in her residence on Obohia Road.

She had become a sewing aide at her uncle's tailoring workshop. It helped her to mingle and run errands for other workers and customers. They were already talking about how Lizzy's waist-side and bust were inviting and her height at about six feet. She could smile all through situations and perhaps the broadest when some of the young men mouthed those "sweet nonsense" about her beauty and bow-like legs.

"She hardly says no; would go many times and come back smiling," one of her neighbours had said. To some, she could be an "easy girl." But "does it worry her?

Doubts... Always smiling, helping people around with such a mind presumably transparent." Of course, with those men, many stories were spawned about how she preferred this one to the other.

Lizzy combined her work with schooling until she completed her primary school education in 1974. She enrolled at the Christ the Lord Commercial Secondary School, on Ngwa Road about three quarters of a kilometre away from her residence. As a day student she battled with school and work at the tailoring shop.

One afternoon, on the third term of her fourth year in the school, 1977, she returned home with a glow and an attitude, like that of a preacher. She was talking to everyone in the shop about going to heaven. Her listeners said she had caught the fever of the new Church movement, "Church *Ogbaru ofuru*." On Igboke's return to the shop that afternoon, she invited him to the verandah, buckled in obeisance, "*Dede*, I want to tell you something very important. Don't be angry, *Dede*. Something has happened to me, a good something; I've seen the light."

"And so...?" Egbuta stared at her. "Hmmm, which light now? What has happened again? Hope you haven't joined these people...?"

"*Dede*, you didn't really know how it was with me, even at Umunnato. Long story! I'm just feeling light, better, *Dee*." Lizzy didn't stop with him. She had spoken to so many people in and outside the yard – neighbours, friends and even casual acquaintances before night fell that day. "What could that mean; what light?" Quite a number in her audience wished to know. Her ready answer, "I was in darkness, didn't know God neither honoured Him. In fact, was going to hell."

"I've accepted Jesus Christ, my Lord and Saviour. It's my new life." That was all that mattered to her. Before her conversion, Igboke had spoken to a few relatives about how that Lizzy followed some young men in the neighbourhood; and worried that often it was said, that "she went on errand." He had made the same complaints in passing to her parents in Amaeke Item. "I don't like her hobnobbing with these stupid boys around here. She has to change and quickly too... otherwise..." He kept quiet for a moment and turned to some of his people who were with him. "She must be suffering from something."

Within the week, Lizzy was already distributing gospel tracts printed A6 size evangelical pamphlets. Her first targets were those men who hung around her, the ones uncle Igboke had called "stupid." From thence, every one of her discussions ended with matters of "Bible study or fellowship."

A group of itinerant gospel preachers had visited her school and preached "repentance, new life in Christ exemplified in good morals and aspiration to live in Heaven," Emeuwa learnt. Lizzy was one of the many young people who had caught the idea of the preachers and had started to pursue some of those activities such as "evangelism."

After checking out things with relatives and friends, uncle Igboke summoned her to give further counsel. "I've received reports of you carrying church on the head. You seemed to have joined those boys and girls talking Church, Church, in this our neighbourhood," he started.

"Well, I'm thinking about the whole thing; seen changes in your conduct; I hope you haven't moved from frying pan to fire, going to these American wonder churches." Igboke could have been one of those who suspected the blossoming Christian evangelical groups that sprouted rapidly after the civil war. It wasn't different from the perception of the evangelical Christian theology of being "born again" at the time. Strong feelings of getting closer to God, praying and singing was on the rise after the civil war. It might have been spurred by the activities of organizations such as the S. U.

Neighbours in the yard had started to speak and debate "drastic changes in her dress style and talks just as some of her classmates wondered about the remarkable improvement in her studies. "Looks like she's even more available at home to help with chores," Uncle Igboke said confirming what his wife had said earlier.

In about six months, Lizzy had become a prominent member of the S.U., the Scripture Union, a non-denominational Christian organization said to have originated from the United Kingdom, UK.

Emeuwa would hear about the new turn in Lizzy's ways and had been discussing with former playmates and uncle Agbai. "Lizzy has acquired a nickname, *Jesus girl*," he said in part. "Maybe, she is just following other people in Aba," some of his mates said. But uncle Agbai laughed, said, "Hmmm, well, what's the meaning? How does that help her...? Will it restore her innocence; the one those soldiers took from her?"

Soon, the news came that "Lizzy will be getting married to 'one big man' who lives in Port-Harcourt; the same place the wedding will take place." The suitor, they claimed, did all the marriage rites in one week. Her parents and relatives travelled from Amaeke to Aba to attend the "high society" wedding. Together with uncle Igboke and wife, they travelled to Port Harcourt. In one hour, they were in the city and traced their way to the venue.

"I haven't seen a wedding so well organised and attended," Igboke said when they returned. They had returned with so many mementoes and gifts after they were hosted separately as in-laws. But Mr and Mrs Egbuta, Lizzy's parents stayed back in Port Harcourt for some days after the ceremonies. They had been so encouraged to take their stay as holidays by Lizzy's new husband and inlaw, Engineer Ogolo Cookeygam.

Chapter Eighteen

On arrival at the partly damaged massive gate of Aba General Hospital, Mama Emeuwa had sighted so many women milling around the premises. They could be in hundreds. It appeared each lapped over her shoulder a baby or strapped one at the back. From their agitated looks, they were in desperate search for medical solution nobody was certain of its availability. Mama, Emeuwa and his younger brother, Onu joined the crowd that gathered at the partly functioning General Hospital. Like those women, Mama was there to get medical solution to the stunted growth and general poor development of her son born during the war. Onu hadn't been able to walk in four years since he was born in 1968. He was smaller than some children of his age — big head, shrunk body with patches of harden skin folds like some other children brought to the hospital. But they were in an environment that was equally sickening - fallen buildings, broken blocks and grass over-grown compound. Everybody's guess was that they were ruined by bombs and other weapons of war that had just ended nearly two years ago. Some of the rubbles were covered by weed and shrubs.

The spared blocks were the ones now in use. At another end, were supposedly vandalized laboratories! Some sets of the equipment looked smoky. They must have been burnt or had taken the colour for lack of use or had come under the weather. The windows and doors of the buildings could have been forced open. Yet, some even feared that undetected land mines could be anywhere underneath the ground apart from reptiles that might crawl out from there.

People conversant with the hospital before the hostilities claimed that some of the workers were yet to return or might not return.

"They might have died in the war," they thought.

The Doctor who could be the Chief Paediatrician was addressing the restless crowd covering the pavement, lawn, car parks and any other available space. But it didn't stop some of the women in the crowd from murmuring. Some of their faces didn't look like people paying attention. "We're sorry that you've waited here for long. There's no way we can attend to all of you today or tomorrow. Our doctors are few; we're just restarting," the Doctor said.

"Not much cause for worry. We've observed that your children, many of them aren't really sick."

"From the number we saw in the past months, they don't seem to have hypothyroidism, that is, underactive thyroid nor do they have cerebral palsy." The crowd became quiet.

"So far, it's that most are suffering malnutrition; as you may know, this hospital hasn't got food to give you, not even enough medicine;" another period of hushed silence.

"We can only advise you for now," said the Doctor in white colour overcoat with stethoscope hanging down his neck. He moved his hands up and down to reinforce what he was explaining. The slight smile on his face was making the women squeeze their faces. Nobody can vouch that they believed him though he was wearing medical doctors' white overcoat and laboured to speak like one in native Igbo and English to drive home his point.

"*Haaaaa…*" the women chorused, loud. Next were multiple chuckles that rose steadily to loud pockets of complaints.

Some of the mothers had started going closer to the elevated point the Doctor was standing, squeezing their faces more like people poised for certain outburst or to pull his clothes perhaps. He pulled back a little and continued.

"We advise that you go home and feed these children with more milk, vegetables, meat, fish and those kinds of food. In three months, you may come back."

"The Pharmacy will give you some multi-vitamins to add."

"*Haaa, onye a o bukwa ezigbo Dokita, is this man a Doctor indeed?*" They asked privately.

"Is it what'll make Onu to grow, walk like a normal child," Mama Emeuwa asked. The other women listening exclaimed, "I wonder ooo; can't this doctor give injection or something?"

Mama Emeuwa wanted to return home with Onu like some women had decided to and headed towards the exit gate. She turned back from the gate saying, "Let me even try this doctor's idea first." If it failed to work, she would continue her search for solution. After waiting for some time, she went to the pharmacy and waited there for another one hour to get the prescribed multivitamins. A few other prescriptions, they bought at their usual chemist shop on Ngwa Road. "One month after, Onu's skin looked fresher; he made a number of feeble attempts to stand up holding chairs and stools," Emeuwa said.

"In the next three months, he was standing and playing with zest unlike months back."

"Before the 3rd quarter of the year, 1972 he walked feebly and progressed thereafter."

As much as the means of Okocha's family could provide, red meat, milk, beans and others became Onu's main meals. Mama Emeuwa didn't go back to the hospital.

Before the hospital visit, she had visited some Chemist shops, and traditional healers. She had thought that since Onu hadn't been able to walk, the baby boy might have more troubles to deal with than the ones they experienced in Amaeke war theatre.

His fate wasn't different from those of many children born during that terrible war period, Mama Emeuwa found out.

Onu was Mama Emeuwa's third child alive. The eldest, Emeuwa at nearly twelve now was three years older than Iroanya Charity, a girl and then Onu. In between the last two were Onukwube and Anyaele, two boys who didn't live long. They had died in succession, a year apart, just before the Nigerian civil war began.

Mama Emeuwa had returned to Aba early in 1972 to join her husband. She spent weeks to settle in and to adjust to the strides of restarting life. Her next desperation was to help her present last child, Onu, to develop and grow normally, the reason why they went to the Aba General Hospital earlier.

With Onu's health and growth issues sorted, she started to give more time to restarting her business of trading used clothes, *Okirika*.

She had been visiting *Ahia Ohuru, New market* regularly as part of her push to sustain the business until she was caught up in the explosion of an undetected landmine that blew up in the part of the market near *Ogbor Osisi*, a reserved portion for timber dealers.

It sparked a fire that raged for about one week. Fire Fighters and Police arrived after some hesitation, battled to reduce the flame and range. Soon, they were bringing out "bodies," according to one of Okocha's family neighbours. He was at the grocery section when the accident happened and was one of the few that went there. According to him, security operatives had created a dump from where a few ambulances were transporting the wounded and bodies to any hospital that was open. Besides, the heap of bodies, were men and women crying, wailing, tearing their clothes and wrapping their arms over their heads. Some had the courage to mope at those wounded and bleeding. Some officials were taking a count of the bodies. Mama Emeuwa was in the number. She laid there with others until somebody said, "her legs are moving." Members of the Police Force quickly brought her out into the waiting ambulance. Off zoomed the Volkswagen bus ambulance, to Nzeribe Hospital about 400 metres away. The few doctors and nurses paced around, discussed in hush tones and began to conduct tests on the relatives who had rushed to the hospital to get a matching blood type. "She must be transfused, needs blood" one of the doctors had said. Mama Emeuwa had bled for the past 45 minutes. Another doctor had started talking about the deep cuts she had and feared that a big vein might have been affected. She fainted and was in that hospital for another 10 days before being transferred to the Aba General Hospital.

Meanwhile, the Municipal government quickly ordered the closure of *Ahia Ohuru*. The Police and soldiers took over the scene and were said to be on the lookout for anymore such landmines. More federal soldiers joined from a detachment in Umungasi. Daily they paraded with certain sets of equipment some said were bomb detectors and detonators.

But Mama Emeuwa's condition had worsened, and the family battled to save her life. Relatives had gone to evacuate her shop and brought back her goods she left there. By November she had stayed in the improvised Intensive Care Unit, ICU of the Aba General Hospital for about two weeks.

Some of the doctors attending to her claimed that she lost a lot of blood on the day of the incident following cuts into her veins. They suspected that she mightn't have had a proper treatment on the day of the incident. Two more days at the hospital, she died.

"After surviving the gruesome war, all those sufferings and devastations in Amaeke; how come..." some neighbours cried with the bereaved family.

Emeuwa and other family members wept for days while neighbours struggled to console him and to talk him out of his heart-rending lamentations.

"Why will she die now; the war is over, the worst is over. Why now?" He kept crying.

"She didn't die when her health was in terrible shape in 1968 through 1969, those days we dodged bullets!"

She was quickly buried amid tears and questions. Emeuwa hadn't stopped to lament.

"Oh God, why now...?

"Is this why you asked me to take note? Couldn't we have written the history together?" Emeuwa cried for days.

Uncle Agbai had come from Port Harcourt to console his elder brother and family. He wouldn't leave soon; he had been with them through thick and thin. He spent more time with Emeuwa and persuaded him to look forward to better days ahead. Agbai had gone to Port-Harcourt from Aba, six months ago.

His promise to take Emeuwa out of Aba to Port-Harcourt, a nearby ports city didn't happen. Papa Emeuwa preferred that his son stayed with him to continue to help with his palm wine bar business.

SEE THROUGH

My eyes conjure the physical in pictures
My five senses shape them into pictures
Giving colour to a vision
Not so plain a version
No matter how I stretch the filtered version
In the eyes of my heart the filters fall off
I see more
Beyond the façade of colour
Of ethnic, racial superiority clamour
All the religious hypocrisy enamoured
And the temporal advantage
In location and geography
Beyond artificial divisions
My heart sees splendour of human diversity
Of colours in intensity
Black, white, red, yellow in sensitivity
In Africa, Americas, Asia and Europe of multi-colours
The same of same in different colours
The same blood of red colour
Brotherhood of diverse colours
Beauty of variety of colours
Beyond camouflague of sensual colours
And the valleys of streams and rivers
Of the Lakes and seas
Pouring tributaries to oceans of many colours
My heart sees through to bliss
In diverse beauty, blushes
Reminiscent of Creator creativity

*Aggregated energy in flowering colours
Mimicking the genius beauty in colours
In the universe of creative colours
I see, I see through.*

Ndu Paul Eke

INDEX

Chapter One *13*
Chapter Two *27*
Chapter Three *41*
Chapter Four *51*
Chapter Five *65*
Chapter Six *71*
Chapter Seven *85*
Chapter Eight *91*
Chapter Nine *99*
Chapter Ten *105*
Chapter Eleven *121*
Chapter Twelve *127*
Chapter Thirteen *143*
Chapter Fourteen *157*
Chapter Fifteen *169*
Chapter Sixteen *183*
Chapter Seventeen *193*
Chapter Eighteen *201*

Printed in the USA
CPSIA information can be obtained
at www.ICGtesting.com
LVHW041509271023
762201LV00013B/1725

9 791220 137348